Queen without Crown

Queen without Crown

By
Madeleine Polland

Illustrated by Herbert Danska

HILLSIDE EDUCATION

Cover and interior book design by Mary Jo Loboda

Cover art by Sean Fitzpatrick

ISBN: 978-1-7331383-5-2

Hillside Education
475 Bidwell Hill Road
Lake Ariel, PA 18436
www.hillsideeducation.com

CONTENTS

MAP OF THE AREA
OF THE WEST
COAST OF IRELAND OFF
WHICH QUEEN GRAINNE
OPERATED HER
PIRATE FLEET.

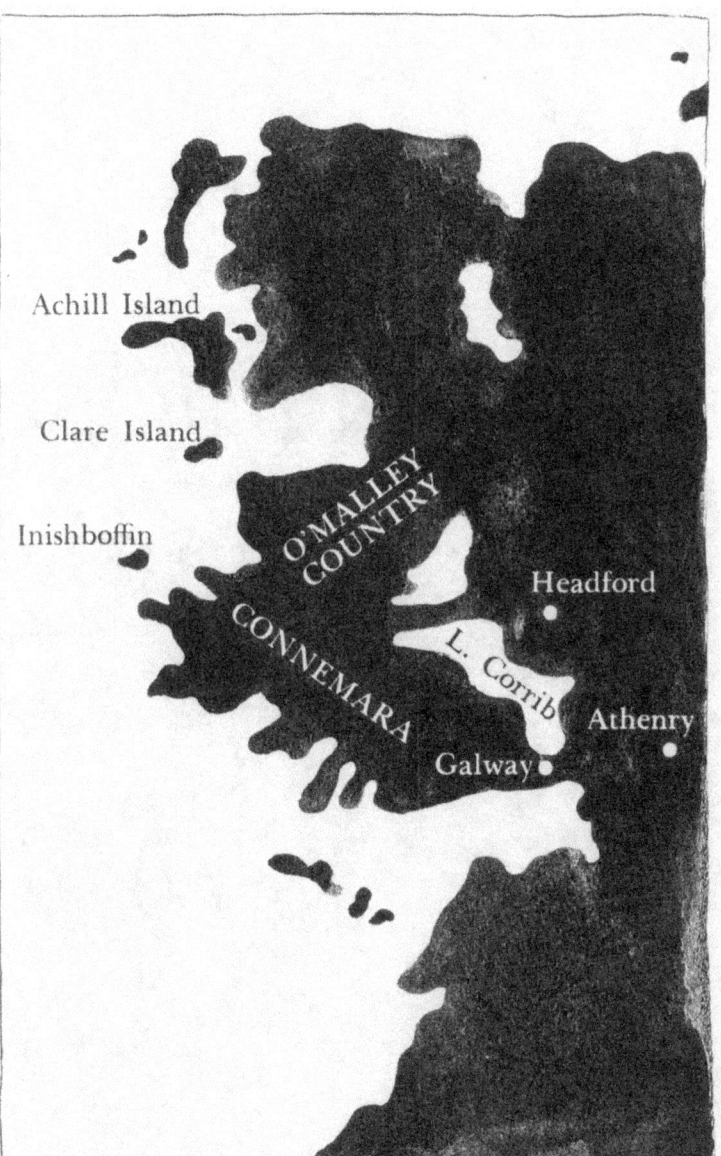

Queen without Crown

Chapter 1

Sunset was scarlet behind the thousand islands of Clew Bay, floating them black on gleaming water that clung to the last light of the day. It glowed in the wings of the seabirds wheeling around the lower slopes of the mountains where the grass ran down into the little pools of the sea, and a boy sat there in the last golden edges of the sun, watching them idly and waiting for the creeping line of shadow at his back to tell him that, for him, night was come. It would be time then to round up and count his father's small flock of sheep, penning them for the dark hours against foxes and even the occasional wolf that strayed sometimes from the inland forests.

He sat very still, thinking of little, not really seeing what he watched but waiting patiently for the cool touch of the

1

shadow, his knees hunched up and drawn tight against his stomach because he was hungry. He was twelve years old and always hungry, thin and overgrown, with awkward hands and feet too big for him, and a head, full of wild dreams, covered by a shock of rough fair hair cropped short in the Irish fashion. Patrick was his name, for his father and for the Saint in the shadow of whose mountain he had been born, but he could never recall being called more than Patch, or Patcheen in soft moments by his sisters.

If he thought at all, it was only of his deep content to be back home again below St. Patrick's mountain, beside the vast, wide silence of the bay, where only the swans and the wheeling gulls troubled the sandy shores below the mountains, and the pine trees leaned in lonely quiet against the Atlantic winds. His father was a freeman, and his family had been so since the old days of the kings, holding their small stretch of lands safe through all the long centuries. Now, in the days of Elizabeth the First of England, Patch's father still held to the old ways and, since the boy was two, he had not lived at home. He had been sent as a foster child to his father's brother, who lived on the flat plains near Athenry, where the wind moaned with the memory of the sea that the child could not forget, and the great Norman keep reared itself above the treetops and above the abbey at its feet. Now he was twelve, his fosterage was over, and he was come back to take his place again within the family that he hardly knew, beside the sea that seemed to him a much closer and unforgotten friend.

The shadows grew and stretched along the hillside and the sheep took on a sudden eerie brilliance in the darkening grass, but the sunset light still flamed over the glittering sea so that his eyes immediately picked on a boat that appeared around the far, terrifying, headland cliffs of Achill. He watched her, black as the islands against the red, fine-weather sky, her sails furled in the windless evening and the small, vigorous sticks of her oars taking her swiftly across the bay toward an island in the middle.

Suddenly the boy sat upright, filled with excitement as the certainty gripped him as to who the owner of the galley was, for he could see now that she was a galley of some size; she must be a wooden ship, she was too large for any of the skin boats of this coast, and it was obvious that she was making for Clare Island! He jumped up, gripped the short grass of the hill with his bare toes, eyes shaded to see better against the low, blinding sun.

"It must be," he cried excitedly to the unheeding sheep. "It must be!"

Clare Island stood out clearly as the largest island in the great sweep of the bay, and one end of it was bluntly crowned with the square keep of Granuaile's Castle, fortress of the O'Malleys of the Isles, rulers of the mainland coast and all the thousand islands of the bay, and of all the larger islands further out to sea. Achill and Inishbofin; Inishturk and Inishmore; all the lonely names of Patch's own lonely world, that had been the world of his family for as long back as word of mouth could tell.

And this must be their Queen coming home to her fortress on Clare Island! Even on the landlocked plains of Athenry, he had heard the stories of the pirate Queen Grainne of the O'Malleys, who sallied forth with her fleet of galleys and skin boats from her island castle, to plunder the ships of the English and the Spaniards sailing up and down her coasts. It was well known that she lent her help to every rebellion against the rule of England, and whisper told that even the great Elizabeth herself listened and waited for the tales of her exploits, and lived in dread as to what ships and valuable cargoes she would lose next to this wild sister Queen on the western shores of her kingdom. For it was well known, too, that Queen Grainne felt herself every bit as mighty as Elizabeth of England, and looked upon her only as her equal.

Patch gave a little crow of sheer excitement, and a sheep lifted its head, still chewing, to look at him in mild astonishment. He was thinking of all the stories he had heard, and hugged himself to think that now he watched Queen Grainne indeed, coming home across the calm waters of her kingdom to her castle at Clare Island. He knew that in the weeks he had been at home, she had not been in Clare Island; away, no doubt, on some gay, plundering voyage, snatching the treasures of the English, and sailing off with a shout of laughter and a snatch of song, with her black hair streaming in the wind. He had heard so much that, like every other boy in Mayo, his fair head was filled with dreams of leaving home and going into her service.

Watching, he knew a moment of furious irritation that he must tend these feeble sheep, while a life like this lay at his very door. Men had come from every corner of Ireland, and gallowglasses across the sea from Scotland, too, to swell her fighting force of two hundred warriors; men who sought a fight wherever they could find one and knew the sword for sport. Adventure beckoned him from the dark hump of Clare Island and from the boat that glided so smoothly toward it on the fading sea. Grainuaille they called the Queen in the Gaelic that was his native tongue and hers, too. It meant "The Ugly One," but this he did not

4

believe; it must mean something else also, for how could she be other than beautiful, this Queen? Strong and fierce with dignity, that she could lead men, as she did, with a crooking of her finger, to the bottom of the sea if need be or to the English gallows on St. Peter's Hill in Galway city. She must be beautiful.

Patch sighed and turned away. He was but newly come home and his father needed him, for his eldest brother, James, was long since gone, and maybe dead, marching off to follow the standard of Ulick and John de Burghe, the wild sons of the Earl of Clanricarde.

They were like Queen Grainne; they would not leave an Englishman alive in Ireland if they could be the ones to kill him. Some part of him was glad that he was too young to have to take a side in these wars, for he longed to follow Grainne and go wherever she might lead, but he could not forget the town of Athenry that he had left, brought to the ground in charred heaps by Ulick de Burghe, who had burned the very Abbey above his mother's tomb rather than that she should rest in peace in an English grave. What good did this do for the Irish, thought Patch, who were left homeless and starving in a ruined town by their own leaders, fighting for some ideal of freedom that would never give the people peace. They said that even Ulick de Burghe and his brother John were starving now themselves, outlawed, little more than beggars, their vast fortunes eaten by their hopeless wars.

The sudden darkness as the sun slipped down into the sea brought Patch to himself. The shining bay had turned to a cold, slatey blue, night was rising from the valley at his back and a cold evening wind whispered through the grass around his ankles. Hastily he turned to his sheep, thinking gratefully that they were not far scattered for he had kept them well together through the day. He was sure he had them all as he waited to count them until they were all together in the pen, resisting the temptation to turn and make for home without counting them at all. Fifteen—sixteen— seventeen. Irritably he hitched himself onto the rough bars of the fold to get above them and counted again carefully, for it was the strange half-light of Irish twilight, and hard to see. He was almost in darkness and yet his eyes were dazzled by the last green light that trembled in the sky above the sea. He could make only seventeen and cursed softly. There was one missing, and now it would be hard to find; he had let it all go late, standing there dreaming of Queen Grainne, and his father would take that as no excuse at all were he to go home and tell him he had lost a sheep.

There had only been pigs for him to mind in Athenry and they looked after themselves, so he knew almost nothing about sheep. He stared around him a little desperately, and in the end, set off hopefully, uphill. Dew was already falling and the grass was cold and wet about his feet. He had no idea where to look. Suddenly the mountain was huge and dark, and not a little threatening. What do you do to call a sheep, he asked himself? And did it answer if it heard you? A pest on silly beasts that could not keep together. He chirruped a little and felt foolish, solitary on the mountain in the cooling darkness. He could feel the ground getting boggy under his feet; wet and full of sinking holes. Heather rasped his ankles and slowed him down. Carefully he zigzagged over the shoulder of the hill, wondering now if he would even find the fold again, or if he and the sheep were to spend the night together on the mountain.

It gave him a fright when he found her. He stumbled

over the sudden white shape in the darkness, a young ewe, little more than a good grown lamb, lying on her side in the heather in utter silence. Silly beast, he thought again, that could not even hear me come. Irritably he thwacked her with his long stick.

"Up," he cried, "stupid one!" He gave her another thwack. "I have had enough of you tonight! Up and to your pen!"

The lamb lay where she was and did not lift her head, and in sudden fear he leaned over her to see if she were dead. A fox? She was too big for a fox to take. He blew a long breath as she stirred to the touch of his hands.

"Up then!" he shouted at her again. "Up, if you are alive!"

Nothing he could do would move her, and in the end he sat down helplessly in the dark heather and peered at her, as though she might tell him what to do.

"What now, my four-footed nuisance! What ails you? What am I to do with you, for I dare not go home without you."

The white blur of wool lay still and did not move and Patch got up.

"You are small help to me," he addressed her severely. "And my father is no more, never telling me what I should do at a time like this! My aunt used to tell the story from the Bible about the shepherd who came home with his lamb on his shoulder, begging all to rejoice with him for he had found the sheep that was lost. I doubt," he added sourly, "that my father will rejoice with *me*, but at least I will bring you home, and we can find what sheep sickness is wrong with you. Now were my mother here, she would bid me stop my endless talking, and get down to *doing!*"

It was not easy. Although she was only this year's lamb, she was heavy enough to take all his strength as he hoisted her on his shoulders and staggered off down the mountain in what he hoped was the direction of his home. Several times he went flying over the tall tufts of heather and the bog holes, he and the sheep rolling hopelessly together down the slope.

"I would like you better," he told her coldly when they fell for the fourth time, and he had sorted himself out from the tangle of wool and legs in complete silence, "I would like you better did you even complain! For all I know I am breaking all your legs, and if I am, then I had better make at once for Athenry, for I need not go home to my father!"

Only the silence answered him, and the far murmur of the sea and a disturbed curlew calling in the darkness. Painfully, he hoisted her up and trudged on.

Why did I not leave her, he thought morosely, and go for help? She would have been safe enough on the mountain at this hour. Now he was no longer on the lonely mountain, but on a track that led around its lower slopes into the town of Newport; people used it, even at night, and he dared not leave her here. He groaned dismally, certain that whatever he did, it would be the wrong thing with his father and, pursing his lips, he tried to whistle to keep his spirits up. But his mouth grew full of wool and he had not enough breath anyway, so he contented himself with cursing the lamb happily underneath his breath with all the words he had learned in Athenry from other swineherds, and never dared to use at home.

What would Queen Grainne do if she were me? he asked himself suddenly, and then decided sadly that she would never get herself into such a mess in the first place. He concluded that she would have little use for him, who could not manage a simple thing like a sick sheep; coming home with his mouth full of wool and the animal probably far worse than when he had found her. Sadly he decided that he was not yet ready to be a hero, and he turned his unstable steps to the side of the track as he saw a light in the distance and caught the soft jingle of harness. Fool that I look, he thought, with this animal slung around my neck. Please be they will not notice me. The track was narrow, running along between the sharp rise of the hill and the sea, and he had to step back, his feet already in the water, to allow the horses to pass.

There were three of them, and they were in no hurry, shambling along the track at little more than a walk, one of them carrying a lantern on a pole. The moon, which was rising by this time, spread a white finger of light along the narrow strip of sea, clearly showing the boy three riders who sat slack and idle in their saddles as if they had little care where they were going. As they drew close to him, he peered at them in the cold, unfriendly light and gasped, partly with surprise, but with not a little fear.

He had no reason to fear, he told himself firmly. Why should he, indeed? But he would rather not have met three English soldiers alone here in this lonely place, and darkness fallen. There is nothing to fear, he told himself again; I have done no wrong. The moon was clear now on their russet coats, glinting on their metal breastplates and the bright pieces of their harness with a light as chilly and unstable as the sudden certainty of danger that gripped Patch's stomach. The first one had seen him, and roughly snatched his walking horse to a stop, as he peered against the moonlight on the sea.

"What have we here?" he cried. "What have we here?" His Irish was bad, but understandable, for most of these soldiers had been in the country for years, living chiefly off the land, and they had learned early that if they wished to bargain for food they must learn Irish to do it, for the resentful people would never learn to speak to them. Patch understood him and, as he looked at them, he understood, too, that for some reason they were all in a bad mood, idle and looking for trouble. Perhaps they had found no pleasure for their evening off in Newport or Westport, and now rode abroad to search for it. The cold snake of fear in his stomach grew larger.

"Who are you and where are you going?" the first one asked. "And what is that you carry?" His voice was rough with authority, and there were badges on his coat and helmet that showed him different from the others.

"Patrick O'Flaherty, sir, and I am going to my father. This is one of his sheep. I found it sick up on the mountain."

There was no reason why they should not believe him, but he knew even as he spoke that they would not. For a moment he thought of dropping the sheep and making a run for it, but the slope of the hill was so steep that he would be no distance before they had pulled one of the firearms that he could see at each saddle. They couldn't miss in the moonlight. On the other side of him, there was the sea, shallow and muddy and the same steep slope on the far side of the inlet. He licked his lips and knew that he must take whatever came, and laughter came first, great gusts of it as they turned to each other and repeated what he had said, and praised it for a story.

"Sick upon the mountain!" they cried and laughed out loud as though they were glad to have anything to laugh at, throwing back their heads and grabbing at their horses that stirred restlessly at the noise. As quickly as he had started, the leader stopped and slid suddenly to the ground, close up to Patch, who could not move back, for his feet were already in the sea, and the sheep around his neck like the ruff of a great lady.

"Where did you steal it?" the soldier asked, and now there was no laughter in his voice. "Where did you steal it?"

Now Patch did step back and almost lost his balance in the rough rocks, so that the man grabbed him by the arm and pulled him back onto the track. He shook him, sheep and all. "Come tell me, boy! Where did you steal it?"

Patch was still dumb, noticing stupidly in the moonlight how the round English faces were unlike any he had ever seen before, being used only to the long faces of his own western country, bred from the Normans and the Spaniards, and even the dark, blue-eyed Vikings of far past times. He realized then what had been said.

"Steal it!" he almost bellowed, maddened suddenly to be so accused when it had taken all his strength to get the animal down the mountain. He wouldn't take that much trouble to steal anything; it wouldn't be worth it. "I didn't steal it! It is my father's sheep and I am taking it home!"

They laughed again.

"Tell that to the hangman!" cried one of them, and they slapped each other's shoulders as though it was a most tremendous jest. But the sergeant, or whatever he was, did not even trouble to answer Patch, leaning over in silence to drag the unprotesting sheep from his shoulders. Patch shook them, aching from the weight, and felt freer and less foolish, and a little braver.

"How dare you say I lie?" he shouted at them, and the dark hills gave back his angry voice, furious that they should laugh at him. "Take me to my father and he will tell you that it is his sheep!"

This seemed to be the funniest thing he had said yet. The leader, laying the inert bulk of the sheep across his saddle front, turned with a sardonic grin, strong white teeth glinting in the moonlight. The other two rocked in their saddles, the lantern bobbing above them, looking at each other as if to ask what kind of a fool this was that they had caught.

"Of course he will, poor simpleton," said one of them. "Of course he will, when he has sent you out to steal it! What else would he say!"

Patch fell silent, outraged and helpless. Enough that they should accuse him; for, after all, was he not there after dark, and the sheep hung around his neck? But there was no answer if they should accuse his father also, for who else could save him?

"Jacob." The leader pushed the inert bulk of the sheep into place. "Do you get off and put the boy up behind John, and tie his hands about his waist." Jacob sprang off willingly, and Patch did not struggle, knowing it was hopeless, for there were three of them, all armed, and he was but a boy. Desperately he tried not to give way to the sick terror that clamored at his stomach, pushing from his mind the memory of those he had seen hanging in the ravaged square in Athenry, after Ulick de Burghe and his gallowglasses were done with it. As he was lifted onto the horse he told himself fiercely that no one could hang him for what he had not done; there must be some magistrate or someone who would believe what he was told. There must be something between him and a death he had not earned.

"Comfortable?" the man asked, sardonically, looking up into the thin face above him that quivered with the determination to show them no fear. "You will have plenty of time to polish that story for the hangman by the time we get to Galway city. But mark you," he added, "we have the sheep."

As they reached the head of the inlet and turned inland onto the road to Galway, Patch twisted his wrists to look back, and the moonlight down the narrow strip of water was like a bright road leading out into the freedom of the bay; to the castle of the Queen on Clare Island.

No one can see me, he thought desperately, when the hot tears came in spite of all his efforts. No one can see me. He bent his head into the shadow of the soldier's back and in a few minutes he had cheered sufficiently to take pleasure in rubbing his cheeks against the shining breastplate, looking with satisfaction at how his tears had dimmed and smeared the polished metal.

By the time he first heard the singing, he was almost asleep, weary with fright and shock, and lulled by the steady clop of the horses; almost able to forget for a while what had happened and where he was going, so strongly did he will himself to believe that none of it was true. When the distant singing roused him, he had no idea of how long they had been riding, jogging along a bog road with the hoofs of their horses noiseless on the soft, dark earth.

On either side, the bog stretched away into the moonlight, as chill and flat and desolate as if they had reached the lost world of the moon itself, and close beside them great drifts of bog cotton moved in the night wind, pale and insubstantial as winter snow. Dimly, in the far distance, they could see the solid shadows of the mountains on the sky. All around them was the silence of the bog, broken only by the rare sad crying of a curlew, which wheeled up into the darkness at the noise of horses.

Into this lonely silence came the singing, faint at first and stopping for a while and then starting again, and stopping; mixed with great gales of men's laughter as it grew closer, strange and ghostly across the vast empty spaces of the dark bog. The three soldiers with their captive began to go a little slower. They looked at each other almost with superstition, and muttered as if they did not know what to do.

"It sounds like a large number," said one of them doubtfully, and the silence afterward said the words he had not spoken; that they were only three, and had no idea who this strange hilarious crowd was, coming toward them through the night. There was no avoiding them by stepping aside into the bog. There was nothing to do but stay where they were and meet them head-on, or else turn and fly the way that they had come. Even the sergeant was holding a little to his horse, but being an obstinate and awkward man, he at once wanted to do the opposite to what the other men suggested.

"They are Irish," said the second one, listening. "They are singing in Irish, and they are many." He began to turn his horse. "Let us get back to somewhere that we can get out of their road."

This was enough for the sergeant.

"You will do as I order," he snapped. "We are the Queen's soldiers. Who are we to give way to any Irish mob! Hold to your road!"

The two others looked at each other and each pale, moonlit face echoed the doubts of the other, and the longing to disobey, but they brought their horses round and faced the way they had been going. Even the sergeant was reluctant to ride on, but sat listening in the darkness, waiting for what might come. Soon Patch was able to hear clearly, pulling painfully at the cord around his wrists to peer past the soldier's back, and even in his desperate plight, he could not but begin to grin and chuckle, understanding the song that was sung. The Englishmen looked at him, and stared into the moonlight, and did not know what to do.

"Tell me," the sergeant barked at Patch. "What is it all about!"

There was little singing now, only broken snatches, and the laughter and the jingling of harness; nothing was yet to be seen.

"All about a fight," said Patch with pleasure, "and torn coats and broken heads and a brandy bottle, and a priest with a long stick and a knife, fighting too, and yelling women and howling boys! A great fight!" Patch grinned happily, forgetting where he was.

"And who were they fighting?" the English soldier demanded sourly, knowing well. "Who were they fighting in the song?"

"Ah—I wouldn't know that," Patch said carefully. "I didn't hear that."

The sergeant looked at him, and then turned away, for the cavalcade was coming closer. There was no sound now save the dull thump of many hoofs and the harness jingle, and suddenly the beautiful sad voice of a woman, which lifted across the dark bog in a little ancient song of love, true and sweet and melancholy, every word clear in the silence.

"I gave you love when we were small and tiny,
And put the crown . . ."

The song came to an abrupt end. The singer had seen the three soldiers in the road, and for a few moments there was no more than the sound of horses, and Patch almost tore his wrists in half to see around the soldier and know what it was all about. The moon was sinking now, but there was still light for him to see quite clearly the company of wild-looking fighting men, perhaps twenty or thirty in all, well mounted and well armed in spite of their fierce and savage looks. At their head rode a woman, and knowing at once who she must be, Patch could only think with foolish disappointment that she could not have been on the boat he saw coming in to Clare Island. For some stupid reason he felt cheated. He should have seen Queen Grainne for the first time on the sea.

Yet he could not but gasp at the strangeness of this encounter, in the forsaken middle of the dark bog, for he never for one second doubted that this was Queen Grainne herself, riding with such authority and arrogance at the head of her men. The Ugly One, he thought, and knew with a prick of sadness that Queen or not, they had named her truly, for she was indeed ugly. Yet there did not seem to be anything actually wrong about her face, just that it was too wild and strong for a woman; and her wide mouth had a strange twist to it, with one long, pointed tooth catching the light where it hooked over her lower lip. Her long black hair streamed to her waist over her cloak with nothing to bind it and, under her skirts, her feet, in rough men's skin shoes, were thrust into great iron stirrups.

She sat there, taller than any of them, in her high-fronted saddle, and stared down at the three English soldiers, and they stared back at her like three mice, trapped without retreat by a hungry cat. She looked them over with her fierce eyes and she said nothing; then she moved a little closer and peered at the sheep across the sergeant's saddle. Her eyes moved and caught the small, fascinated face peering from behind the second soldier. She edged up her horse, taking no heed of the Englishmen who stared in astonished silence, until she was beside Patch, and again he nearly tore his hands off in order to turn and look at her.

"And what, by all the bones on Tara," Queen Grainne said to him, "put an Irishman like you into company like this!"

Chapter 2

The English sergeant did his best to hold to his dignity.

"None of your business, madam," he cried, "who the boy is! May I ask in turn who you are, riding with this armed band at night? What is your business? You threaten the peace of the Queen's Realm!"

Towards the end of his brave sentence his voice faltered and grew a little foolish, wilting under the fierce hawk eyes that stared at him from below the wild black hair; eyes filled with derisive laughter and contempt, as though she said aloud to him that well enough he knew who she was, and not to trouble her with his bravado.

" 'Tis the Queen's Realm indeed," was all she said, with a small snort of laughter, and then she turned back to the wide-eyed boy.

"Who are you?" she asked again. "And how did you get into the hands of these foreign fools?"

Patch could hear the sergeant rumbling with fury as he answered.

"Patrick O'Flaherty, madam," he told her, "of Coolinbawn, down there at the back of Newport."

"O'Flaherty," Queen Grainne said after him. "O'Flaherty. A grand name to own." In the pale fading light, the harsh face grew strangely gentle. "A grand name. 'Twas my own for a while."

Her first husband had been Donal O'Flaherty of Ballynahinch, her young love of the song, and her husband when they were little more than children. Patch was too shy to tell her that his father, Fergus, was far cousin to her dead husband; he could only stare at her from behind the soldier with wide, fascinated eyes. The gentleness left her face.

"And why, my young O'Flaherty, I asked you," she said, "have you let these round-faced English get you here trussed like a fowl?"

Patch gaped. How could he have stopped them? Before he could frame his indignant protests, the sergeant tried again.

"It is none of your affair, madam, whoever you may be." Foolishly he failed to see the hard, dangerous glint in the long-lashed eyes that watched them all. For those who knew her pleasure, the smoke-blue eyes of Queen Grainne were her greatest beauty; to her enemies they grew hard and cold and gray as the slate hills of her native Connemara. "He is a felon," went on the Englishman, "taken in the act of sheep stealing. We take him to Galway for justice. Clear your men, madam, and let us pass."

Grainne did not even seem to notice him; she bent close again to Patch.

"Felon are you?" She laughed. "Was it an English sheep?"

"No!" cried the boy furiously. As bad to be accused of stealing an English sheep as an Irish one, when he had stolen no sheep at all. "No, I am *not* a felon. It was my father's sheep and I was taking it home!"

"In the black of night!" one of the soldiers said sarcastically, and Queen Grainne laughed again. She seemed to believe him as little as the soldiers did, and he did not know who he resented more. She was of his people, and should believe him.

The English sergeant lost his patience, infuriated by this wild-looking female who ignored him and his authority as completely as if he were not there at all.

"Begone, madam," he said, "and leave us to our business!" and as he spoke he reached for his sword.

Patch could never quite remember what happened next. He saw the quick stripe of light that was the drawn sword in the moonlight, but almost before it had cleared the scabbard, the Irish warriors who had been sitting idle and amused at a little distance had flashed into movement as fast as the sword itself, and in seconds they were all round Patch and the three soldiers. There was almost no noise; a few grunts and snarls and frightened whinnies from the horses, and the heavy thump of a body falling. It was the Queen, herself, who caught the man as he toppled in front of Patch, between his ribs a cutlass that had left a long cut on the boy's hands as it went in. She held the two of them against her weight, bawling for someone to come and cut the boy free; then she let the dead man slide to the ground and turned a wide, mischievous grin on the astonished boy where he still sat behind the saddle.

"Begone, madam," she cried then, in the high English voice of the sergeant, and the men around her roared with laughter. "Begone, madam!" She looked down at the sprawled body. "He'll not tell Grainne O'Malley to begone again, nor anyone else for that matter! Into the bog with them!"

Patch rubbed his raw wrists, and sucked at the blood that flowed from the cutlass nick, and stared at her, thinking of his imagined picture of a tall stately queen. Somehow in the dim, cold light, she looked a little less than human, strange and ugly and a little terrifying, and then she turned suddenly and smiled at him, close and friendly; he blinked as though a light had been kindled that brought him warmth as well as brightness, and he stared again and wondered how a moment back he had been almost frightened.

"Are you well, Patrick O'Flaherty?" she said, and Patch beamed back, bemused, into the warmth of the splendid eyes, and the astonishing sweetness of the smile that so transformed her ugly face. Why would he not be bemused, young boy that he was, faced with the charm of Queen Grainne, for which most of the men behind her would have ridden gladly to their deaths. "I am well, madam," he said, "and I thank you."

"Good," said Grainne, and that was the end of the matter. "Now we are wasting the hours of the moon for riding." She did not appear to give a second thought to the three dead men that had splashed quietly into the bog. "Take that horse, boy, and take your sheep since you took the trouble to steal it, and get back to your Coolinbawn."

"But I didn't," cried Patch. "I didn't steal it! It is my father's truly. I did *not* steal it! I *would* not steal it!" She turned back again, with that compelling trick of offering him her complete attention, and looked into his face in the darkening night.

"Does it matter?" she asked him, and the rather raucous

voice was quiet. "Does it matter to you, whether I think you stole a sheep or not?"

Tears were trembling on the edge of Patch's lashes. "Of course it matters! I would not steal a sheep, and it is not simply that 1 fear the noose!" He was desperate that she should believe him. It was of no account what these Englishmen had thought, but he could not bear that Queen Grainne of all his dreams should set him on his way, and then no doubt laugh heartily, with all her men, to see him a felon so young. He did not stop to think that Queen Grainne herself was the most cheerful and unthinking felon on the whole coast of Connemara, with a price on her head from the English Queen. "Of course it matters!"

"Then I believe you. You did not steal the sheep." She laid a hand a moment on the thick thatch of his fair hair. "I would not like my son to be a felon either." Her voice brisked up. "But now, boy, if you want to live to see another honest day, let us be gone. Take that horse, and you may ride with us as far as Newport, but then turn it loose before the town, or you will be charged with stealing the horse as well as the sheep, and that would be a good night's work for the size of you!" The men laughed again, and a pair of hands helped him into the saddle, and another lifted the stirrups until they met his dangling feet. Knowing the Queen wanted to make haste, he did not dare to say that he had never ridden a horse alone before, his uncle being too poor to own one, and the two old things belonging to his father being only for the plow. He felt alone up in the air, and unsafe and anxious, and he was glad when one of the men threw the sheep across the saddle front, and said, "There, boy, your father will be waiting for it!" He did not mind the ripple of laughter that followed, for what matter if these men did not believe him as long as the Queen herself did. It helped to have the woolly bulk in front of him, filling what seemed to be vast spaces on which he could slip about the horse's back.

Somehow he had managed to hang on till Newport, clinging to the reins and the thick wool in front of him, joggled and bumped by the trotting horse, so that he stood breathless with his legs like jelly underneath him when at last, in the outskirts of the rambling town, they told him to get off. It was pitch dark by now, the bitter blinding dark of the hours before the dawn, and yet these men and their tall, strange Queen seemed to know the country as if the sun shone from beyond the mountains. They rode confidently away when they had whipped his horse loose.

"God give you safe home, Patrick O'Flaherty," the Queen had said, and he had screwed his eyes in the dark to see her face, knowing from the sound of her voice that she meant it. "If they get after you again," she added, "you can always take refuge in my castle! It'd take more than the English to get you out of there!" Patch did not know how to answer her, for how did you answer a Queen, even one like Grainne, who as everyone said, was truly like no Queen that ever was.

"God give you safe to Clare Island, madam, he said in the end, and he could sense her smile in the darkness.

He had not risked going through the town, where even in the dead of night there might be an English patrol, and he did not want to be caught for the second time. With tired and mulish obstinacy he clung to the sheep that could be the only thing to get him into trouble. He had *not* stolen it, so why should he abandon his father's sheep just to please these English; not that he even knew by now whether the animal was alive or dead. At the thought of death, he felt a twinge of fright, remembering the soft splash of the bodies in the bog, but resolutely he put it from him. That was the Queen's affair, and in any case, who would ever know? The bog did not yield its secrets. He staggered on carefully through the fields outside the town, making for the farm homestead on the other side of it, far from the grazing grounds on the mountain, for the land around the house was too soft for sheep, who must needs be kept on the higher ground.

It was worse than the journey down the mountain, stumbling into bog pools till the icy water reached his waist; butting into thorn trees and tangling with the gorse bushes, talking all the time to the sheep as if she was his companion in misfortune.

"Though for all I know," he said to her, climbing wearily from a bog pool and pulling her after him, a solid mass of wet wool that made her twice her weight. "For all I know, you are long dead already, and I am breaking my shoulders for nothing!"

He sat down to rest when he felt himself on firmer ground, and thought, unless he had gone wrong, that he should be on the shoulder of the valley where lay his father's farm, with Newport lying a little below him and between him and the sea. It was getting towards dawn, and while there was yet no light, there was a faint stirring of the air above the still silent earth, telling of the coming sun. He felt the cold wind on his wet shirt, and longed desperately for his breakfast, looking down almost without interest at first, at the sudden springing of lights down in the town below him. Torches were moving in the streets, and in the dead silence of the last dark, he heard the thrumming of hoofbeats along the track between the hills that led to his father's farm, and on out into the forsaken wastes of Connemara.

He was desperately tired and a little stupid, given over completely to his strange, foolish journey with the sheep, lost to all other thoughts except that he must finish it, and hand over to his father what was his. This was somehow all the more important since he had been accused of being a thief. He remembered the warm, vital face of Queen Grainne as she assured him that she thought him honest and, remembering it, he smiled a little foolishly, only to be caught in the same moment by the cold sick thrust of fear. In his weary stupidity, it had never occurred to him to think that the sudden stir below in the town might have anything to do with him. Now he watched and knew a sense of certain danger in those moving lights, and the hoofbeats that had gone drumming past on the track below.

"Oh no," he whispered. "No."

It could not be true, he told himself. How could they know where to go, even if they had found the dead soldiers on the road, and how could they have done that when the bog would swallow them like a hungry bird? Yet there was clearly trouble of some kind, and the hoofs had gone out towards his father's farm. He put his head on his knees and prayed. Enough for him to be taken on suspicion of killing a sheep or stealing it, but there were dead men out there in the bog, and his name had been given, and no gallows were high enough for those who killed the English and were caught. But who could, or would have told? None of the Queen's men for certain, for that would be to hang themselves as well, and in any case she would not try to shift the blame for such a thing. She would tell the English she had done it, and then defy them to come and get her; all the garrison of Galway city had tried to capture her some few years back, and she had laughed at them from her island castle, harassing them until they were forced to go home and leave her where she was. No, it would not be Queen Grainne. He calmed himself and tried to think it out, and in the end he could not see how anyone could have known of it, and he decided that the uproar in the town and the horsemen out in the valley must have been for something else.

As he came to this comforting conclusion, the high cone of St. Patrick's mountain was touched with the first gilt of the sun, although the land behind lay still in the gray shadow of the dawn. He roused himself to go on to the last stage of his strange night's journey, calm now to the point of looking forward to the warmth of the hearth fire, and the shirt drying on his back while he told them of his adventure. But some deeper fear made him cautious, and he came very carefully around the shoulder of the hill that gave him his first view of the farm below him, sheltered in the fold of the hill itself.

In the instant he dropped to his face on the ground, throwing himself flat and flinging the sheep away, trying to hide from sight in the long grass that waved gently in the first wind of dawn. Then he made himself lift his head carefully and look again. Gray daylight was spreading through the soft, green valley, and like a dream in the unreal light, he could see his family, from the father down to the smallest one that clung weeping with fright to her mother's neck. The russet coats of the soldiers looked dark and heavy in the dead light, but the first brightness touched their helmets and their pikes driven into the ground while they strung the family on a knotted rope as if they herded them to market. They looked all around them when this was done, and walked once more in and out of the house, as if they searched for someone else. Then they hustled them away, banging them along with the flat blades of their swords.

They moved away down the hill, and one soldier turned back with an almost casual gesture, and laid his torch up against the low thatch of the roof, smoke pouring out on the instant, darker gray than the new light of the morning, and followed by the eager lick of scarlet flames which paled suddenly as the sun came up over the mountains and flooded the whole valley with the day. Watching, Patch felt the touch of sudden warmth on his face, and around him, larks flung themselves singing into the bright sky.

"No," he said despairingly aloud, against a solid thickness in his throat, looking down at a world that for him might as well have been still wrapped in darkness. "No! I did not even steal the sheep, and they did not kill the soldiers!" He almost stood up and raced down the hill, to clutch those russet coats and cry at them to leave the family be for it was none of their doing, but he held back, clinging to the long grass until he tore it from its roots, knowing he would save nothing and only add himself to the procession for the gallows.

He did not know how long he went on lying there after the small, sad group had vanished along the valley track, sprawled with his face buried in the sweet grass that warmed under the sun, the sheep beside him with its filmed eyes showing it already long since dead. The dreadful night had been for nothing, and he did not turn or even move when much later in the day, a hand was laid on his shoulder. The sun was high above the mountain flank and the blue shadow creeping down its western side. What matter if they did take him now with all the others.

"Patch," whispered a voice. "Patch. Don't sit up now, whatever you do; just turn your head to me. I'm sorry for your trouble and I have food for you."

He turned then, dull, indifferent eyes on a boy of his own age who lay flat on the grass beside him, a dark cloth bound round the fierce thatch of red hair that would have been a beacon to anyone watching from below.

"How did you know I was here?" he asked him, his mind refusing to allow him to ask questions about what had happened in the valley. "How did you find me, Sean?"

"I saw you," Sean said, and his whisper was filled with pride. "Just for a second as you came over the hill this morning. I came all the way around to get to you, for those devils are watching still, and if we as much as blink, they'll have us! Turn around now without lifting a hair on your head and eat what I've brought you, and we'll make a plan."

The steady murmur of the other boy's voice was calming, and in a moment Patch did what he was told, knowing as soon as he tasted the rough wheaten bread that he was ravenously hungry.

"Sean," he said at last, urgently, "how did they find out? Who told them?"

"Well, Patch, man." Sean's voice was hoarse with admiration and his blue eyes roved over Patch almost as if he never seen him before. It was clear that he would far rather be asking the questions. "Well, in God's name you have some tale to tell yourself, but whatever happened to you, they found this creature crawling out of the bog on the road to Galway last night or this early morning, and about six wounds in him, every one as big as a basin. But before he died, didn't he tell them that it was Patrick O'Flaherty of Coolinbawn that did for him. Did you honest, Patch? Did you kill an English soldier?"

Wearily Patch put his face down in the grass again.

"I did not," he said flatly, and Sean's face fell. Had he crawled all the way around the mountain with the bread, and the fellow O'Flaherty no hero at all when he got here? He almost snatched back the piece of food from Patch's hand.

"Queen Grainne killed him," Patch said then. "Or her men did."

His voice was as weary and lifeless as he was himself, but his words had Sean quivering again with excitement.

"Queen Grainne?" he hissed, and had to make a conscious effort not to shout. "Grainne! Ah, Patch, you're making it all up! Tell me what happened. Why did she kill the soldiers?"

His bright blue eyes were fixed on Patch in doubt and awe; ready to listen and longing to believe. Patch tried to steady his mind on the strange events of that long, long night that already seemed behind him like a bad dream, but there was nothing dreamlike about the spirals of dark gray smoke that still rose idly from the sunken, blackened heap that had been his home. Nor about the russet coats that glowed like autumn trees here and there about the valley, where the soldiers guarded the track, watching all ways into the farm, lest he should come home again. He turned to where the flies gathered over the dead sheep.

"They said that I had stolen a sheep," he said slowly.

"And Queen Grainne killed them?" Sean asked, and his eyes wide as saucers.

Patch closed his eyes.

"Queen Grainne thought she killed them," he said, thinking of the one who crawled out of the bog.

Sean had nothing to say for a moment.

"Ah, to be sure," he said then, and his voice was filled with admiration. "She'd be glad of the excuse."

"What'll you do now? Where'll you go now, Patch?" he asked after a while. He had crept over the hill full of big plans of feeding Patch, and then making some big plot between the two of them, with himself very much the leader, and saving Patch from the gallows. But he lay now in the grass and looked at the weary face of the boy beside him, seeing it years older than the one from which he had got a cheery grin only yesterday morning when he met Patch on his way to tend the sheep. He listened to the hoarse, tired voice telling of strange, wild adventures in the night, and naming the pirate

Queen Grainne O'Malley as if Patch knew her for a friend. The Patch that he had known was suddenly gone from him, and he felt young and small and helpless. Patch did not need him, and he knew it.

"What'll you do now, Patch?" he asked again, humbly.

Patch opened his eyes then, and looked at him fully, and the tiredness was dropped from him.

"I am going to Queen Grainne," he said firmly. "She told me to. As soon as it is dark and I can get off the hill, I am going to Grainne." He looked at his friend, and saw something of his forsaken feeling in his subdued freckled face. Cautiously he leaned over and put a hand on his shoulder.

"Thanks, Sean, for the bread," he said, and dumbly Sean nodded. He knew that it was all that he could do.

Chapter 3

It had not occurred to him that Queen Grainne would guard the sea around her island fortress as grimly and securely as the Anglo-Normans had guarded the walls of the great keep at Athenry, nor had it occurred to him that the journey would be so long. He stole a boat where he had once noticed it, lying unguarded in the simple trust of the holy men at the little quay of the abbey of Murrisk, and the path of moonlight seemed clear and simple across the sea to Clare Island and the castle of the Queen.

It had already been a long walk across the hills to Murrisk, and in no time at all his arms were stiff and worn from the unfamiliar oars, yet each time he looked across his shoulder, the shadow of the island seemed no nearer. The night was calm, and the sea smooth and whispering like silk, yet it was all he could do to hold the light boat from going in circles, turning him back with the sweep of the incoming tide towards the mass of tiny islets and the lonely, curlew-haunted sandflats at the inner end of the bay; back into the hands of the English soldiers.

Panic began to take him. His arms were tearing from their sockets and he made no progress, and in the end he was crying silently and helplessly, struggling alone on the great glimmering sheet of water, aware of nothing at all but his desperate attempts to keep the boat headed for Clare Island; hearing nothing in the wide night but the uneven splashing of his own oars; gulping the salt tears into his mouth because he did not dare to loose a hand to wipe them away.

Queen Grainne's watchers took him unawares, as they swept the bay in their long curragh; alert to every movement on its dark surface, they bore down on the small boat to see who it was that crept at night towards her castle. Patch stared in stupefaction as they drew alongside him, the soft rhythm of their oars drowned by his own untidy splashing, and he did not move as a hand reached out and grasped his gunwale.

"Brian's bones, but it's a child," said the man who had leaned over. "Where are you off to, boy?"

Patch did not stop to question who they were. Even in the wavering sea light, he could see from the rough beards and cropped hair that he was among the Irish.

"Queen Grainne," he said, and eased his red-hot palms against the oars. "I must get to Queen Grainne."

"You try to row to the island by yourself?"

"Yes, yes, I must get to the Queen."

"Did you not know it was nine sea miles? A day's good rowing for a man!"

Patch shook his head, for he had not paused to think

how far it might be. The romantic fortress, black against the glowing sunset, had seemed but a stone's throw across the water.

He looked dumbly all round the rough faces in the boat, and one of them peered suddenly.

"We took you from the English last night, boy," he said. "On the bog road with a stolen sheep!"

Patch was too weary to protest, nor did the sheep seem to matter any more.

"They are after me again," he said urgently, hoarse with fatigue. "One of them was not dead, and crawled up from the bog and told my name, and they have taken all my family and burned my home, and I did not even take the sheep nor kill the soldiers!" His voice rose. "I must get to Queen Grainne, and she must save my family."

The two boats rocked gently in the darkness and the sea slapped against their skin sides, and in the silence the men looked at him and at each other.

"He's only a lad," said the one who had spoken first. "We cannot send him back to hang for this. 'Twas I killed one of them."

" 'Twas maybe you," said another, "that did not do the job properly, and let the Englishman live to tell the tale!"

"All the more reason I wouldn't let the boy hang."

He turned back to Patch, his hand still a white glimmer on the gunwale.

"I wouldn't count now on the Queen being able to save your family. She's not in the best position for treating with the English at the moment!" There was a rumble of laughter through the long boat, as the men thought of the expedition from which they had just come back; a fine game of cat and mouse with an English ship trying to get in to the garrison in Galway. By the time Grainne was done with her, she rode higher in the water, and there was not much left for the garrison in her plundered holds. "No, boy, the English would not listen to her now about your sheep—but she would not have us throw you to them all the same. Another mouth to feed in the castle will be neither here nor there, and I daresay you can scrub a deck as well as any."

Patch nodded limply. It was almost without thought that he had tramped over the deserted hilltops and seized the boat in the darkness at Murrisk, driven by instinct to search for help in the only place he could think to look for it. Now he stared in silence at the rows of bearded faces in the other boat, trying to grasp reality; that these were indeed the Sea Queen's men, whose shadowed faces looked at him kindly if with a growing impatience, and who offered him shelter and work on the legendary island of their mistress. In spite of his grief and horror at the morning's work, a sudden surge of excitement gripped him.

"Come, then," said the one who held the boat, "what are you waiting for? Ship your oars and jump over." They sat him down in the middle of the benches and he watched as they lifted his little curragh from the water and propped it in the stern of the big one.

"Whose is the boat, boy? Where did you get it?" one of them asked suddenly and, as he told them, he could feel the murmur of disapproval through the length of the curragh.

"We must take it back tomorrow," said the leader. "Father Abbot of Murrisk is long friend to Queen Grainne and her dead father. No quicker way to earn her anger than to steal from the Abbot."

Patch felt there was something wrong in picking and choosing from whom you would steal, but he was too content to think of it much, as he hugged his aching arms and felt fear slide from his mind in the warmth and safety of the two men like walls on either side of him, the shafts of their oars weaving steadily in their big hands. It was his second night without sleep, and gradually the paling moon and the heaving sea and the large moving hands drifted all together into a darkness shot with the memory of flames and soldiers and his baby sister crying in his mother's arms; but before sorrow could take him they all swam away into the strange, ugly face of Queen Grainne, fierce with strength to give him armor against the English, and with its odd tenderness that was an armor against his grief. There was nothing more until, in the pitch dark that comes before the day, he woke with a jerk as the curragh bumped against the quay at Clare Island.

There were thrown ropes and the careful shipping of oars and men's voices all around him in the blackness, and a torch flaring high against a rough stone wall immediately above the sea. The water smelled very strong here, and the boat was rising and falling in a way that made him glad to be getting out of it. Dimly he saw several other curraghs, and the outline of bigger ships, then a hand on his neck was pushing him firmly up a flight of steep steps, slippery under his feet, and he stumbled over a doorsill nearly as high as himself into a vast room where a couple of lads were lighting candles on a table and laying down food. Beyond the small glow of candlelight and the dying fire in the great stone hearth the vast, cold room was wrapped in shadows and the beamed ceiling seemed to the boy's drowsy eyes to stretch away up into nowhere. He vaguely saw the sleeping men around the floor, wrapped in their cloaks, some of them stirring and cursing at the cold breath of air from the night outside. Then one of the lads kicked a log into flames and added another, and a hand shoved Patch into a seat beside them; a bowl of soup and hot brown bread, sweet from the oven, was thrust before him. No one seemed to care who he was or why he was there, or whether he had any right to the Queen's food. The poor of Grainne's island kingdom would have told him that in the Queen's care he would fare as well as she did herself, dependent only on the supply of Spanish wine ships and English merchantmen who fell to her marauding galleys. Almost before he was at the bottom of the bowl, he was asleep again, rolling to the floor amongst the men; nor did he hear them rising all around him in the morning save as a vague storm of noise that did not trouble his sleep.

It was late morning when he finally awoke and climbed out over the sill of the door. The sun was already high on the familiar slopes of St. Patrick's mountain, the pointed cone hidden by the little crown of mist that told of clouds to come. On a green meadow towards the center of the island, the men seemed to be holding some sort of games, wrestling and racing and jumping, the gallowglasses from Scotland flashing their bare shins. The long quay where all the boats were moored was on the sheltered side of the castle and alongside it ran a large paved area that sloped at one end into the sea. Men were calking an up-ended curragh, and Patch sniffed with pleasure at the smell of salt and tar, pungent in the sun. There were men working here and there all over the boats, even on two strange wooden ones with tall masts, but nowhere could he see the two who had brought him to the island last night, and indeed he was not sure if he would know them again if he saw them. And where was Queen Grainne?

As during the night before, no one took any notice of him. The men whistled and sang at their work in the bright, tar-smelling sun, with the cool salty air blowing in off the great sweep of water that spread seemingly to the ends of the world, surrounding and almost overwhelming the small green island. Patch thought he had never seen so much sea in all his life, and he also thought he had never been so hungry, but it was beginning to dawn on him that in this place, if he did not care for himself, he would find no one else to care for him. And he had work to do. Mixed with the gasping excitement of finding himself, in truth, on the magic island at which he had stared so wistfully only two days ago, was the sore, terrible memory of what had sent him here. He had need of Queen Grainne and must find her, but first he must find food.

He found the kitchen easily enough, by following the smell of roasting meat across the great hall, empty now except for a few old men whittling sticks on the seats about the fire. He found himself in a low, smoke-darkened room built onto the side wall of the keep, where an old woman bent a benign scarlet face above a sheep she roasted on a spit, which turned and whined in a fireplace as big as a small kitchen in itself. At a square pitted table, four kitchen lads were chopping herbs, and the smell of baking bread was sweet and hot against the meat. Patch licked his lips and almost held his stomach in his hunger; he did not know what to do, for no one here paid him any more attention than on the shore. And where was Queen Grainne? Did she truly, then, keep state in her castle as he had first supposed, far away from her men in some lonely magnificence?

"I'm hungry," he said in a loud voice that seemed to him to fly all around the stone walls like the croaking of a raven, and at the spit the old woman slowly straightened herself, and the boys turned grinning from the table.

"It was only your tongue was needed to tell us," the old woman said equably. "How else would we know?"

Patch stared bewildered as she walked to a press against the wall and took out a round, brown loaf, the flaked oatmeal drifted gray and fresh across the top of it. She found a knife and a piece of cheese and finally, with slow, unhurried movements, dipped a beaker into a pannikin of milk and set them all before him on the table. Did they behave thus to every stranger that came? he thought, watching in astonishment. He could not settle to eat, starving though he was, without some words.

"Do you not want to know who I am?" he asked. "Do you feed me and not care whether I have a right to your food?" His face was bewildered.

The old woman paused at that and really looked at him, shrewd, narrow blue eyes peering from the creases of her flushed cheeks below a slightly crooked cap, and her arms folding themselves across an apron that was none too clean. She heaved gently with laughter that spread over all the wrinkles of her face, and the boys at the table grinned too.

"Why should I care, shockhead?" she said, and Patch lifted a hand to his hair. "Should I care?"

"No—no—but perhaps I should not be here. I may be an enemy." He was troubled. Could any stranger come to this island fortress and be taken for granted as he had been? It was not safe for the Queen.

They all laughed out loud and looked at him, thin as a scarecrow after two days of hunger, his clothes bedraggled from their soaking, and his thatch of fair hair on end.

"To be sure," the old woman cried, as if it was the best of jests. "You could be an enemy!"

"God save Queen Grainne!" cried one of the boys in mock terror, and the old woman took pity on him.

"No one reaches this island, son, unless my lady Grainne shall wish it."

"She does not know I am here."

The sandy eyebrows lifted.

"Then how did you come?"

Delighted at last to have found someone interested enough to listen, Patch told his story, but when he came to the part about being picked up in the curragh, the mild curiosity faded from the woman's face and she nodded, ready to go back to her spit.

"If Owen brought you," she said, "then that will be right with my lady."

"But I must see her!" Patch grew urgent. "I must see Queen Grainne and get her to save my family. She must tell the English that it was nothing to do with them—or me!"

Now there was the same moment of attention that there had been in the boat last night, and then the same murmur of laughter. The old red face that looked down at the boy was sardonic.

"I doubt me, shockhead," she said, "that the English would listen to her at the moment. If it is a friend of the English you want, then you have come to the wrong place."

Patch began to plead, but she was already turning away.

"You are quite safe here, boy, and I promise no one will molest you, nor will any English soldier reach you." She chuckled hoarsely. "They have tried, but my lady does not like them on her island!" She picked up her great pewter spoon. "Now eat your victuals, for the good God knows you look as if you need them."

Patch could not hold back to argue any longer; he crammed the good food into himself, as though he might never see more. Excitement rose as his appetite was satisfied, and grief faded a little under the bright pleasure of being where he was, in the castle on Clare Island, the home and fortress of Queen Grainne herself. He sat up on his stool and squared his skinny chest, hiccuping a little, and faced the room as fiercely as any of the other men who locked each other in their deadly grips, out on the salt-swept fields.

"Where can I find the Queen?" he asked truculently, and the old woman stopped and looked at him.

"Leave the Queen alone, shockhead," she said. "She and her husband, Master Richard, have great things to decide."

She laughed comfortably. "Or Master Richard thinks he has. Leave her be, I tell you, and go out and see what work your idle fingers can find to do among the ships."

Patch banged on the table in his anxiety.

"My family! I must see her to get my family safe."

"Thank God you have yourself safe, and leave it at that!" The old woman was growing irritable. "Or maybe you'll take a boat and row yourself back to the English! Get out of my kitchen now, and from under my feet! Shoo!" She flapped at him with her apron as she would at a rambling hen, and mutinously Patch obeyed her, stalking from the kitchen with what dignity he could muster under the eyes of the grinning boys. Having taken all this trouble to reach Grainne, he was not going to be kept from her by some red-faced hag who treated him like a child. He stood in the chilly spaces of the hall where the old men still whittled their sticks and the only sound was the mournful crying of the seagulls beyond the door; slowly his temper cooled and he began to use his mind.

This was a plain square of a keep, this castle, and it was clear that the men lived in this lower room, built onto the rocks above the sea, with the high stone sill to hold back the water that swept up even there at the highest tides. So the Queen must obviously have her rooms of state upstairs. Though, 'pon my soul, thought Patch, she lives in great silence. Around a Queen, he thought vaguely, there should be trumpets blowing and people rushing here and there to carry out her orders. He was a little troubled that it had not been like that on the road, but he told himself that when she rode at war, it must needs be different.

He found the stairs quite simply, in the corner of the hall, winding up into the thickness of the wall, and he looked guiltily over his shoulder as he set foot on the lowest step; but no one watched him, nor did men-at- arms threaten him from above with tasseled spears, nor gorgeous angry servants rush down to tell him to be gone. Queen Grainne did not trouble with servants or sentries at the entry of her private quarters, but neither, Patch discovered as he reached the door, did she live in silence. He was faced with the huge oaken door, studded with great nails as large as the palm of his own hand, and even as he leaned against it in hope of some clue as to what went on inside, he heard Queen Grainne begin to laugh, gale after gale of helpless laughter, infectious, so that he smiled too, his cheek against the wood. Against the laughter, he could hear the faint, affronted voice of a man who clearly disapproved.

Left alone to grow into the feeling that he belonged there, Patch had gained courage in his morning on Clare Island. He had gained courage too from his moonlight meeting with the fabulous Queen Grainne, and the sudden gentleness of her wild, ugly face; and who could fear this laughter? Carefully he raised the heavy iron latch, and pushed the door open a little, standing still to peer into the room, where, as he had grown accustomed in this castle fortress, none lifted their eyes to look at him, too intent on what they did themselves.

Chapter 4

The room was perhaps less than half of the hall below it, and state room or not, it was clearly the private chamber of the Queen herself. She sat in a high-backed chair of bog oak as black as her own hair, her hands along the arms of it and her head thrown back against the red velvet of its cushions, as she showed all her crooked teeth in helpless laughter at the tall man who stood between her and the fire. Weakly she took the end of her yellow linen sleeve and wiped the tears of laughter from her eyes, and in the next second she sobered. When she spoke, her voice was like a whip.

"I think you lose your senses, M'William Eughter," she said, using her husband's most formal title. "I think you lose your senses to come to me with such a thought! I, Grainne

O'Malley, Queen of all the Isles!"

"Her Majesty," the man answered, in a stiff tone that matched his strange, unbending way of standing, "Queen Elizabeth of England is Queen of all the Isles of Britain. Excepting, madam, those of your own kingdom," he added hastily, seeing the dangerous burning of his wife's eyes.

Grainne reached for a snuffbox from the table beside her, pale, ancient gold, finely carved in the old, old patterns of her kingdom. Over the lifted lid she eyed him as she sniffed the sharp black powder, a dusty trail falling down the front of her dress.

"And what is it to me, Richard Burke"—and this time she gave him his name—"who or what Elizabeth of England rules? Is she not just another Queen exactly as myself?" Her voice was dangerously soft, and the eyes over the snapped lid were dark as slate.

The man before her looked down from his stiff height. For all their cold and formal talk, he was her second husband, Richard Burke, Chieftain of all the Burkes in that western county, the M'William Eughter, loyal Anglo-Norman knight, in willing service to his Queen, Elizabeth of England. Later, Patch was to come to know him like everybody else, as Iron Dick, since he hated to wear armor, and owed his high, stiff carriage to the steel vest he always wore underneath his doublet, pretending he wore nothing. He was to come to know, too, as much as he could understand it, of the fierce pull of loyalties between this strange and ill-matched couple, who could not do without each other, and could yet find almost nothing on which they could agree.

"A slightly larger kingdom, madam," Richard said now, treading warily, for he knew the danger signs in Grainne's eyes. "A slightly larger kingdom and I do not doubt that if, as I suggest, you offered your allegiance to Her Majesty, she would treat you with all the respect due to your rank."

Grainne's deep, disgusted sniff was only partly due to the pricking of the snuff.

"She would do me too much honor, the woman would," she said tartly. "Who am I to ask anything of Elizabeth of England; respect or anything else either! If she wants me and my allegiance, let her come and get me!"

She cackled abruptly, a sudden and almost childlike laugh of pure mischief, and the cold gray eyes grew a soft and sudden blue. Two huge tawny wolfhounds that sprawled across her feet lifted their heads for a moment at the sound, and one of them turned idly to lick her bare foot before he laid his head down on it and slept again. The bright, mischievous eyes blazed at Richard Burke from between their curtain of black lashes.

"Tell her," she said again, "to come and seek me if she wants me. But tell her this time to come herself, and not send those poor lads from Galway to cut themselves to pieces against my rocks. Then maybe the boot'll be on the other foot, and I'll do her a bit of honor in my own castle!"

Carefully Richard Burke held his temper. One wrong word to this wild, provocative, hot-tempered wife of his, and she was capable of ceasing her laughter and calling for her men, to sweep out and show him who was Queen of the Islands of Murrisk, with some mad attack on some English ship. He eased a fine handkerchief from his ruffled sleeve and mopped his damp forehead. She was capable, by God, if he should annoy her, of loading up her boats with her pack of cutthroats and sailing on the next tide to slaughter Queen Elizabeth in Greenwich Palace. Nor would he like to be sure she could not do it; thumping up the quays in her bare feet, her long black hair streaming out behind her, and the O'Malley war cry screaming on her lips, so that enemies fell back before her from sheer amazement.

He moistened his lips and prepared to try again, for he was sure that he was right. These ancient rulers of Ireland, like Queen Grainne, and like himself, were now all at odds with each other. Every small stretch of land under its own ruler demanded a different set of laws and different tributes and taxes. These stripped the poor of all they had, and stripped the rich, too, for they were forever fighting each other for what they thought to be their rights. He had no more use for Queen Elizabeth than Grainne; she meant nothing to this far corner of her kingdom. But Iron Dick, like most reasonable men, was sure there would be no peace for this sad and ravaged land until it was all gathered under one rule; and the rule of England was as good as any other.

"Think of our people, madam," he said as patiently as he could. "They are starving while we wage wars above their heads."

Grainne fixed him with a cold, ferocious stare.

"There is no one starving in the Barony of Murrisk, M'William," she said frigidly, "but I am told about it and send them food. Look to your own lands if the people are hungry there, and give them food, as I do. I wage my wars *for* my people, and see that they enjoy the profits!"

For a moment the long, bearded face of Richard Burke looked helpless and defeated, and watching him through his small crack in the door, listening in silent fascination, Patch was reminded sharply of the dead face of the sheep, lying beside him in the long grass on the hillside. Then Iron Dick came back to the attack, and the mild face composed itself.

"I am not thinking only of your lands, madam," he said,

"where no doubt you care for your people well." He did not point out that she cared for them with plunder from the ships of England. "I am speaking of Ireland as a whole. If we are to save this land of ours, it is time we learned to be as one, and to cease to war among ourselves."

Grainne, sniffing noisily from the snuff, and wiping her nose unashamedly on the back of her hand, had not taken her eyes off him. Iron Dick made a move as if to offer her his handkerchief, and then thought better of it, and pushed it back into his sleeve, but the small gesture did not escape Grainne, and the dark eyes flamed for a second.

"You may well put it away, Richard Burke, for I have no use for such fripperies. As to the rest of Ireland— that is in the care of your good friend my sister Queen who, you tell me, rules it! Bid her then to feed her people! Do not waste time talking to me about it; go talk to my sister Queen as you talk to me, bidding her to do this and that, and see how long, my good Richard, you would stay outside an English jail! Why tell me that the people of her lands are starving. The people of my lands and isles are *not!*"

Again Iron Dick bit back the answer that she fed them with the stolen goods of what she called her sister Queen. No English ship was safe along that coast of Ireland, nor had been for many years. But there was a lot at stake at this moment and he would not allow himself to annoy her; he must not, if he wished to win into Elizabeth's service not only all her ships and the men who went with them, but also Grainne herself. She wielded a strange, almost superstitious power over all this part of Ireland, and if Grainne and her seamen and her soldiers and gallowglasses became loyal to Elizabeth, it would do more to settle this war-torn, ravaged country than any other thing. Patiently he answered her again.

"*Your* people do not starve. But what of all those who are homeless and starving at the hands of your friends, whom you help with men and money because you say they fight for Ireland. Men and money for the two mad sons of Clanricarde that they might lay waste the town of Athenry, burning and destroying homes and crops, rich and poor alike, so that there is no home left standing, no animal in byre or field, no stalk of corn to ripen on the whole plain of Athenry. What, madam, has this done for Ireland? Other than kill the children that should be its future."

This last thrust was cruel, and this Richard knew, for the oddly tender heart that lay under Grainne's wildness could never resist the needs of a child. She stared back at him in baffled dismay, her long fingers twisting in the ends of her hair.

"How do we know this is true?" she cried defiantly. "All this is said of my friends John and Ulick, but is it true? We have only heard tell, and people make these stories wild, to be better telling around the hearth fires in the winter. How do we know these things are true of Athenry? Who has seen it?"

This was too much for Patch. He did not know who the tall man was, but he had put into words all the things that had been restless in his own head since he had stood before his uncle's door, a safe distance from the doomed town of Athenry, watching over the flat green fields as the smoke rolled in gray clouds fringed with scarlet from the small, prosperous township. It had risen over the square ramparts of the castle where my lord of Bermingham and his soldiers made their desperate defense; it had risen in the end even over the high pointed gables of the abbey church itself.

Patch was so deeply involved in what he heard that he had totally forgotten where he was, ready only to plunge into the argument on the side he felt so desperately to be right. He thrust open the heavy door, dragging at the rushes on the floor, and rushed without thought into the middle of the room.

"It is true, madam," he said urgently, without greeting or respect or beginning of any kind. "It is true what —what— what the gentleman says of Athenry. I saw it! I was there! They came sweeping down at dawn, and we were all safe and well, and no one minded being ruled by my lord of Bermingham, for he is an old man and good. We were well enough as we were, but my lords of Clanricarde and their men destroyed the whole town, and my lord Ulick in the end set fire even to the abbey where his mother had her grave, saying that it were better than that she should sleep in peace with the English! And it is true about the children, madam, for I heard the people tell of it when they were gone. My uncle would not let us go into the town for days, but I heard the people say when they were gone— about the children—they—they—"

He could not tell her what he had heard that they did to the children in the name of Ireland, not then nor ever after could he speak of it. He faltered to a stop, and the dumb horror of what he had heard filled his gray eyes as he stood and stared at her. But there was no surprise on her face or on the face of Iron Dick; faced with the truth of what they discussed, they had not paused to ask who it was that brought it, unannounced.

Gradually the spell died, and Patch shook himself and came back to the present, looking in sudden doubt and fear into the faces of the two grown-ups. What had he done, bursting in like this? Queen Grainne would be so angry that she would never help him now. She sat up slowly in her chair and pushed away the bodies of her two dogs, limp against her feet in their contented sleep.

"And who are you," she said, "to tell the truth to Grainne O'Malley?" Before he could answer her, amused recognition dawned on her face. "I know indeed! You are Patrick O'Flaherty of Coolinbawn, who would not steal a sheep, English or Irish." She looked him up and down, from the thatch of tow-colored hair to the bare feet wriggling uncomfortably in the rushes, and her eyes were warm. "A man of truth, obviously, Patrick O'Flaherty, and honor."

He thought she teased him, in her rich, sardonic voice with its western lilt, but he could not be sure, and a warm flush crept up his face until it was almost as scarlet as the flannel of the Queen's kirtle. But he gripped the floor firmly with his toes and clamped his lips together, his fair head coming up to meet her eyes steadily.

"I hope so, madam," he managed to say, and would not give her an inch for laughing at him. The Queen's smile broadened, with a glance at her husband as if to say, see the young one, see how he fights me! Richard Burke merely looked down from his stiff, iron-bound height, no expression on his long face, only anxious to get rid of this bothersome boy as soon as possible and continue his vital conversation with his wife. But he knew her well enough to see that for some reason she was taken with the child, and that if he showed any wish to be rid of him, then the willful woman was capable of holding him there beside her all day, so that further talk would be impossible. So he stood quiet, his light eyes on the sea beyond the windows, over which the sun was failing and the clouds, promised by the small crown on St. Patrick's mountain, were gathering in from the ocean.

Grainne had forgotten him and Elizabeth of England, always ready to turn from anything to give her interest to a child; always ready to warm to anyone, man or boy, who had the courage to look her in the eyes and give her word for word.

"And tell me, Patrick O'Flaherty, how you are come to be on Clare Island? I sent you back last night to your father with the sheep you did not steal."

Patch wished she would stop talking about the sheep. It was enough once he had made it clear he had not stolen it; why could she not leave it at that? Her teasing eyes when she spoke of it made him feel uncomfortable, but he looked at the snuff trail down her dress, and told himself a Queen should be more clean, and that gave him courage to start his tale of what he found when he reached the hill above his home.

As when he told the tale of Athenry, he was soon taken by the strength of his own feelings, and words came easily to him as they came to all the people of this western land. His gray eyes fixed in entreaty on the Queen's. He forgot to notice Grainne, as he told her what had happened to his family.

"So you see, madam, you *must* help them! They did not kill these soldiers, but your men did, and I know they did it for me, and I thank you, madam, for your help, but it is not right my family should hang for this thing. And madam, I did not even steal the sheep in the first place!"

This time Queen Grainne did not laugh.

"I know, boy," she said, almost absently. "I know."

Even Iron Dick was listening now, his vague eyes withdrawn from the cooling sea and a frown of disapproval between his brows as he looked at his wife, waiting for her to explain this latest caper. She seemed a little uncomfortable and avoided his eyes.

"Where did they take them?" she asked, clearly playing for time before she must give an answer, and Patch shrugged in slight exasperation.

"How could I know? Will it not be Newport jail?"

A bare, angry foot suddenly kicked the two wolfhounds out of the way in a scramble of brown fur and long stumbling legs, and Grainne was on her feet, pacing the length of the chamber with her rough scarlet skirts swirling around her and her shawl gathering up the rushes as it trailed behind her on the floor. At the far end she stopped and gazed out of the window as her husband had done, even in her preoccupation casting one quick, expert glance over the changing weather. Then she suddenly whirled back.

"Go down now, Patrick O'Flaherty," she said, "and find yourself a place to eat at my table, and a place to sleep beside my fire. You are safe here and will want for nothing, and no Englishman will get you out of *my* hands."

Patch looked from her to her husband, and longed to be able to leave it at that, more than a little terrified by the Grainne who swept up and down the room with her black brows drawn down over her eyes like thunder and her wide mouth tight clamped as a trap. At the moment she looked very much The Ugly One, and it took all his courage to hold his ground and speak.

"But, madam," he said and his voice came out all thin and high. "But, madam"—and he managed better—"that is not enough. You cannot let my family hang for what your men did. It is no use to me to be safe if they are dead and it is all my fault."

He managed to get to the end of it, without turning and running from the furious blaze of the slate gray eyes, but he was startled and encouraged to catch a faint and approving smile on the face of Iron Dick, as he looked from one of them to the other. Queen Grainne soon dealt with his daring.

"Begone!" she roared at him, and a bare foot slapped down into the rushes and Patch hardly knew how he reached the open door. "Begone down where you belong, and think yourself lucky to get that!" As he reached the stairs in his headlong flight, she called again. "Stop! Come back!" Patch crept back, but only just as far as the door, where he could be ready for instant flight. Nor did he speak, but waited under the fierce glare that pinned him where he stood. When she spoke, after a long time, her voice was curiously gentle.

"I am grieved about your family, Patrick O'Flaherty, and you did not have to say it again. Now go on down and I make you no promises."

As soon as he was gone, Richard Burke moved over and closed the heavy door.

"Grainne," he said, but he only said it to a mutinous back, for she looked out again over the sea, from where a cold wind blew now, stirring the long strands of her black hair around her forehead. "Grainne, why can you not leave them alone?"

"The English, is it?" Grainne asked him sharply. "Why should I leave them alone, and they in my country?"

Richard sighed.

"You had a small army with you last night. You could have got the boy and the sheep and killed no one."

"They'd have come after him."

"If you hadn't made him shout his name all across the bog, he could have come here exactly as he has done, and no one the wiser, and his family would have come to no harm."

She turned from the window and her dark face was bleak with irritation. She might secretly be stricken with guilt for thoughtless trouble to the child and she might criticize herself: but no one else must ever criticize her. Least of all that long-faced Anglo-Norman there by the fire, looking down his nose at her and telling her to leave his English friends alone.

"The man was cheeky," she snarled. "Like all Englishmen! Keep your preaching, sir, that you cannot allow me a prank!"

"A prank!" Iron Dick looked even more rigid than his own armor. "It is pranks from you and from your friends, the Clanricardes and their like, that are costing Ireland her peace."

Grainne stuck out her long neck and made a face at him. Then she drew herself up to mimic his own rigid manner.

"A prank!" She echoed exactly his shocked voice. Then she flew at him and stamped, as she had flown at Patch a few moments earlier. "Well, Richard Burke, such pranks as I care to commit inside my own lands are my own business and none of yours, and I'll thank you to keep your judgments!"

It was her husband's greatest weapon against her that she could never ruffle him.

"And the boy's family?" he asked her, ignoring all the rest and knowing he hit where it hurt. "What of them?"

She wheeled on him. "That is none of your business either, M'William Eughter." She set him at a distance by using his formal title, but her eyes were unhappy behind her fury, and Richard Burke knew his wild Grainne. Carefully he changed the subject, going back to their original conversation that the boy had interrupted.

"You will think, madam, won't you, of what I have been saying? Sir Henry Sidney rides into Galway in October, in his progress around Ireland to settle her complaints. They say he is a good man and wise. You could do well to offer him your lands and men in fealty as I will myself, getting them back then in the name of the Queen. I hear that many of the Irish Chieftains plan to do this, O'Flaherty, O'Kelly, O'Naughton, and many more. Think on it, madam, if, as you say, you care so much for Ireland."

Grainne had not moved as he spoke. Her eyes, still dark with anger, were fixed on him and she did not answer for a long time after he had finished speaking.

"I will think on it," she said then, and there was nothing to be learned from her voice. Richard bowed and left her chamber, followed by a dark, fierce glare that promised him no good.

She sat down in her tall chair and stretched her bare feet out before her, hitching her skirts up to the heat of the fire, for the room was growing chilly with the cold wind from the sea. Her face was dark as the gathering clouds beyond the window, and she stared brooding into the sinking logs, ignoring even the cold, loving nose of one of the dogs who came and thrust it into her hand.

She was still sitting there when Owen came into the room; Owen O'Flaherty, first cousin of her own dead Donal, and in command now of all her fleet of ships and her small, fierce army.

"Enter," she said sharply when the knock came at the door, but she did not move nor lift her eyes from the fire until Owen stood beside her chair, his thick mat of black curls still damp from the sweat of his morning's exercise.

"Well, Owen," said his Queen sourly. "Do you come too to try and persuade me to pick up my skirts and curtsy to the English Queen!"

Owen looked mildly astonished, but he was well accustomed to the extravagances of Queen Grainne. Nothing to her was ever of small importance; either she was lost in gloom or riding high on a whirlwind of high spirits. He did not even trouble to ask her if she spoke seriously; his mind was full of the news he brought himself.

"I would not waste my breath, madam," he said, "to try and persuade you into such foolishness. Did I try, you might feel it your duty to ignore the English galleon due to pass Achill Head before dawn. She has been in Derry and Sligo Bay, and rumor has it that she carries gold to pay the garrisons around the coast, and she is due to call next in Galway. If my Queen is not too friendly with Elizabeth of England, then we might try to find out if it be true that this ship carries gold!"

He was grinning now, and Grainne looked up at him out of the corners of her eyes, his own grin spreading to her.

"We could that, Owen boy," she said. "We could check on what she carried, and that should please M'William, for I would only be watching what went past my own door, lest there be any harm in it."

She sat up briskly in her chair, and life and sparkle returned to her face, banishing the moodiness.

"With what escort, Owen?" Now she was down to business.

"Two, madam," he said. "She must be laden with something worth having."

"True for you." Grainne scratched her head vigorously, leaving the black hair standing in a tangle. "We'll take the two galleys," she said thoughtfully. "And half a dozen curraghs to play the goat with them with the lanterns on poles, so that they'll not know how many ships we have at all. We'll drop on them just before dawn." She lifted herself on her arms and took one expert glance out the window. "We'll drop on them an hour before dawn a little north of Achill, and the tide'll be just right to take them in and wreck them on the Head if we leave them crippled." She laughed and her eyes were bright with mischief. "We can tell my sister Queen that we were very sorry to have them run onto Achill Head while we checked to see if everything was in order. Will that do, Owen?"

Owen's rawboned Connemara face reflected her own devilish grin, his long mouth stretched and his gray eyes bright with malicious pleasure.

"That will do well, madam," he said. "Well enough indeed. Little we thought to have another crack at the English so soon."

"Little we thought," she echoed, and got up to move over and stare out critically at the sea that served her so well. The clouds were low now and covering the sky, obscuring the mountains around the far shores of the bay, and the flat, quiet sea of the morning seemed to have swelled up to ten times its size, gray and solid, heaving in with a sullen roar against the seaward cliffs of the island.

"Will it hold, Owen?" she asked.

"Long enough," Owen answered and he, too, came and looked long at the sky and sea. "Long enough, but I'd say we'd better be in the shelter of the bay soon after dawn tomorrow. But it'll hold long enough for the task in hand."

Grainne turned suddenly as if she dismissed the weather and the sea as of no more importance, and threw open a chest against the wall; a long, wooden chest, heavily carved with hinges and locks of ancient gold. For a long moment she stood silent, looking at the folded clothes inside it, rich with the soft odor of musk.

"Go down, Owen," she cried, "and tell old Honor in the kitchen that my nose speaks to me of a sheep roasting there.

Tell her to serve it well, and do it credit, for I am dining in my hall today. I have a mind to be a Queen when I sit down to my table, and Elizabeth of England shall be no finer. Tell Honor to come to me when she is ready, for I will need her help."

But when Owen had left her, the smile faded again from her face and her eyes grew dark as she brooded on the heavy water.

"A Queen tonight," she said to herself, "and tomorrow I shall think. Tomorrow." She looked across the cold sea that was as much her kingdom as the green fields of England were kingdom to Elizabeth. "My own kingdom, you say, M'William, or else the welfare of my people; you say I must choose between them, and I love them both." She shook herself with a sudden irritation. "A pest on small O'Flaherties and all those like them," she cried aloud. "Why can they not look after themselves and leave me to my ships!" She slapped across to the door in her bare feet, and flung it back with a crash on its hinges.

"Honor!" she bawled down the dark stone stairway. "Honor!" All through the square castle, men raised their heads and grinned, affection and admiration in their faces. Their Queen was on the rampage about something, and when she was, then all had better hoist their storm sails and look out for squalls.

There were no squalls in sight when Queen Grainne came into the hall on her husband's arm at the hour for dinner; when the dull, declining day gave no light through the narrow slits of windows, and candles blazed in all the sconces on the walls and down the rough timber of the tables. The chairs of Grainne and Iron Dick, handsomely carved from oak as black and deep as the bog it came from, were the only things of beauty in the uncouth and warlike room, but on a sudden impulse, Grainne had bidden Honor delve into the chests for the ancient treasures of her family, which she had never valued before except to sell them piece by piece if she ran short of money for arms and equipment for her warriors. She wore a kirtle of crimson velvet, covered by a cloak of finest lamb's wool, bleached from the skins of the young lambs that frolicked on the green fields above the sea. Her black hair was sleeked and shining from the efforts of the astonished Honor, and crowned with a thin fillet of gold, worn by the ancient ladies of the O'Malleys, far back in the days of the kings. Around her weatherbeaten neck lay a chain of gold, so heavy that it bit into her shoulders with its weight, and jewels winked and glimmered at her brown wrists. Her feet were awkward in soft unaccustomed shoes of calfskin, and as she stepped proudly in them to her place at the top table, the long face of Iron Dick at her side was filled with a mild astonished pleasure; surprise so took her followers that silence fell all over the crowded hall, and every man's face was turned to her in stark amazement. Queen Grainne forgot her splendid dignity.

"What are you staring at, you crowd of dolts?" she shouted at them. "Have you never seen your Queen before?" She stood and glared at them until they turned back shamefaced to their tables, and as she sat down, spreading her crimson skirts with satisfaction, she looked all around her.

"Where is the boy?" she asked. "Where is Patrick O'Flaherty, who came unasked to my island?"

Patch was still terrified, rent completely now from his dream of a quiet and dignified Queen; realizing that you could never know when the blast of her lightning could fall from what seemed like a clear blue sky. He stood up diffidently in the low place that he had found for himself, but he dared not speak.

"Where is he?" the Queen shouted, peering down through the smoke and turf reek into the shadows of the hall.

"Here, madam, here," shouted the men on either side of him, and before he could even speak, they hoisted him up onto the table in the middle of the bread and candles and wine cups, above a sea of huge, bearded faces that seemed twice the size of life, grinning up at him in long endless rows.

"Send him up," cried Grainne, clapping her hands, and they slapped him on his ankles and bade him walk, his head swimming with the height and the heat of the candles on his legs; trying to put his feet between the food and the candlesticks and to ignore the jests. From the far end of the table, the bright, dark eyes of his Queen blazed out at him from below her golden crown, but she knew she had teased him long enough, and when he reached her, his feet straddling a joint of her sweet-smelling mutton, she bade a man to lift him down at once.

"Well, Patrick O'Flaherty," she said then. "Are you still my friend?"

Patch longed to say, "Only if you will help my family," but he did not dare, and also he knew already that it would not be the truth.

"Yes, madam," he said, knowing as he looked into the ugly, charming face so close to his, that no matter what she did or did not do, no matter how she frightened him, he could never refuse to be her friend if she would let him. "Yes, madam," he said breathlessly. "I am your friend."

"Good," she said. "Then you shall be my page. I have heard that my sister Queen in England has a boy she calls a page, who stands beside her and holds the plate for her meat, and then, in God's name, a bowl of water to wash her fingers!

Now why she would want that I shall never know, but if she can have it then so can I, and you are the very boy to hold it for me."

She drew herself up, determined to be every inch a Queen as great as her sister across the water, and by her side, her patient, exasperated, devoted husband looked at her with his mild blue eyes, clearly wondering what new nonsense was this from his wild and wayward wife. All down the tables of the men stared at her and hoped there might not be too much of this, for Grainne of the Ships was a fine master to work and fight for, but if there was much of this grand lady business, they would not know where they were.

They all of them mellowed with the flow of good ale, and of Spanish wine taken with their own hands from passing ships, and as the evening faded into darkness over the swelling sea they forgot their doubts, and Grainne forgot much of her determination to be a proper Queen.

"Sing for us, madam," they cried, as they always did when she dined with them and the meal was past. Behind her, the bewildered Patch stood with his little bowl of water and a towel and did not know where to put them, for the Queen had forgotten and had no use for them. "Sing for us, Grainne," the men cried, calling her by her name in spite of the disapproving face of Iron Dick, for they loved her and that was why they fought for her, even unto death. "Sing for us!"

She smiled and swept past them in her crimson skirts with her cloak trailing in the rushes, to where her gilded harp stood waiting at the fire; and from the tables they turned as one man to watch her. For want of anything better to do with it, Patch drank his little bowl of water and then threw the bowl into a corner, and there was none to see or care.

Little sad songs she sang them first, of her lost love and the white blossom on the moorland and the sadness of autumn, and the lost promises of love; and the smoke rose silent to the blackened rafters above their spellbound faces. But she knew not to hold them too long, sweeping suddenly into the O'Malley Rant, which Patch had heard that evening in the bog, her rapt face breaking into a grin and wild mischief dancing in her eyes. Tension broke, and sadness, and one by one they sang with her until the roar of men's voices rocked the very stones, and Grainne watched them and knew them in the hollow of her hands; and she spared a moment to pity the Englishmen, coming round the steep cliffs of Achill in the dawn. Then she turned away from her harp and clapped her hands for the piper, who wailed up into the old tunes of the islands, and the men leaped from the tables, pushing them aside to make space for the ancient patterns of the warlike dances that in past days had been for men alone. Grainne kicked off her skin shoes, and gathered up her velvet skirts, footing it among them under the narrowed, doubting eyes of her husband, still in his place at the end of the top table. In his corner, wild with the excitement of the singing men, and the fierce music of the pipes, Patch danced alone, footing it too among the rushes with his eyes smarting from the smoke and his towel waving round his head, page to Queen Grainne O'Malley.

They were all still dancing there, with the night black as pitch above the sea outside, when Owen pushed his way through them to the Queen's side, and whispered to her that it was time he bade the men to go.

Chapter 5

G rainne stopped in mid-step, and the music wailed down to a stop and, at a sign from Owen, the men began to melt immediately from the hall. Patch came to as abrupt a stop as the rest of them, his face flushed and his eyes bright, confused by the sudden stop to the revels, but still filled with the excitement of having entered the wild, fierce world of Queen Grainne, that had so tempted him two evenings ago across the shining bay. He had already forgotten that he had expected anything different from a Queen. "What is it? Where is everybody going?" He plucked at the sleeve of the man who passed him closest.

There were no secrets on Grainne's island, for everybody

down to the lowest scullion gave her absolute allegiance, and so could be trusted to know what was afoot. The man looked down at the boy from under a thick tangle of dark red hair, one of the gallowglasses from Scotland, with his plaided kilt swinging above his bare shins.

"English," he said briefly, a wild light of pleasure in his bright blue eyes, for apart from the prospect of a fight, the Queen was generous in her sharing of the spoils. "A pay ship for the troops, heading for Galway. We'll take her off Achill." He was away before Patch could ask any more, but in his excitement, in the middle of this crowd of pleased and purposeful men, he forgot all his doubts and fears about the rightness of the wars, or the wisdom of the endless fighting. He was on Clare Island, in the Queen's own castle, and she was making ready to sail out against the English, and by the bones of St. Patrick, he was going too!

He had to struggle for his breath a moment in sheer excitement and nervous fear; it would be a lesser task to go out against the English than to approach this terrifying Queen, but he gulped deeply and marched across the floor to where she stood at the end of the empty table with Owen and her captains, a sea chart spread among the toppled wine cups; though they had little need of charts, for they knew each current of these dangerous seas as Elizabeth of England would know her gardens at Greenwich Palace.

"Madam," said Patch, hugely and bravely at her elbow, and as she turned sharply at the interruption, he nearly ran away. "Madam," he bellowed in his nervousness. "What would the page of Elizabeth of England do when she went into battle?"

Grainne looked at him, and around her the men grinned amiably at the skinny, determined boy. There was always calm and certainty when her raids were planned, for every man knew his task backwards, and there was no place for anxiety and short tempers. The Queen stared into the frightened but fierce gray eyes that glared nervously into hers, and then she laughed out loud, showing all her crooked teeth, and banged Patch on the back so that he almost fell across the table.

"I daresay, my proud warrior," she said, "that he goes with her and carries her cutlass or her blunderbuss, though I am told," she added disparagingly, "that Elizabeth of England is not one to go forth and fight herself, but sits in scented comfort with a little dog, and lets her menfolk do her fighting for her. But you are page to Grainne of the Isles, and shall follow her to war! Yes?" she added after all her big words, looking down into his face as if to say, and is this what you want, you poor little fellow, and if it is, you shall have it?

Patch could not speak for the feeling that choked his throat. He nodded his fair head vigorously, and told himself that it was not fear that stopped him speaking, for was not this exactly what he had wanted?

"Then wait for me at my ship," she said, "and now begone, for the tide waits not even for me."

Iron Dick did not go with them, but watched somberly from his place before the hall fire, as if he knew the hopelessness of trying to talk this wild pirate into loyalty to her sister Queen. When he had first married her, drawn irresistibly to everything in her that was so different to himself, she had been a widow, left in poverty by the death of her young husband, whose lands and money all went to his own family. She had returned to Clare Island with her handful of followers, and with wide innocent eyes hiding under their black lashes she assured her new husband that she had taken to piracy again only because she would otherwise have starved, for how else could she have lived? But now they were three years married, and Iron Dick was rich, so that Grainne need lack for nothing; yet she still went racing out to sea to trap every passing ship that seemed worth the robbing. He could not even get her to settle in his own home in Burrishoole, but if he wished to live with her he must stay in this barbarous castle on her island full of cutthroats.

Yet when she came to bid him farewell before she went out to the jetty, he said no word against her, but bent his head stiffly for her kiss, and asked God for her safety; looking sadly into the blazing, excited eyes so close to his own. As well to try and change the tides of the sea, as to change his Grainne.

There was no sadness about Grainne herself as she whirled out of the hall, jumping over the high doorsill with her bare legs flashing under the dark brown skirts girdled short about her knees. She wore a light metal breastplate, painted black, and close dark sleeves to her wrists. She seemed determined not to forget Patch.

"Here," she said to him where he stood beside the door. "Here, page!" She hooted with laughter. "Do your duty by your Queen." She tossed him a heavy cutlass on a wide leather belt and sheath so studded and ornamented that he staggered back against the wall as he caught it, and it was all he could do to haul the weight after him over the doorsill. But his temper was rising against this Queen, and he was determined to show her he was not the humorous weakling she obviously thought him. Flinging the belt across his shoulder to take some of the weight, he followed her out into the flaring torchlight of the quays, where most of the men were already waiting in the boats, and the lights shone greasy in the heaving sea.

"The soot, Owen," said Grainne and, even as she spoke,

Patch saw to his amazement that the face and hands of every man were blackened, so that they were no more than shadows where the torchlight did not fall on them. He watched with astonishment as the Queen dipped her hands into a bowl that Owen held, rubbing it all over her own face and merging herself into the night in her dark clothes. She handed it on to him, and he stood and looked at it.

"Must all the expedition wait on Patrick O'Flaherty?" she asked sharply, and he gave his face a few tentative rubs, until she seized the soot in irritation and almost took the skin off him.

"Why?" he asked, trying to keep the smarting tears from his eyelashes as she rubbed his hands.

"Why?" she echoed. "Would you have me write a letter and tell them that we are coming? We will be over their rails in the dark before they even know that we are on the sea."

Patch hitched the great weight of the cutlass on his shoulder, and padded after her as she went on board one of the big wooden ships. The night was very dark and filled with the salt smell of the sea, that swelled steadily and blackly away into the night with no white wave tips to break the endless darkness. The wind drove from the ocean, steady and not too strong, but out in the black distance there was a threatening whine to it, as if warning them not to take its quietness for granted. He stuck closely to the Queen for he was terrified that otherwise he might be in somebody's way— every space on the open deck was packed with fighting men, no more than shadows in the night with their blackened faces and dulled weapons. Grainne was quite right. They slid across the swell under taut black sails, and in the darkness in their darkened clothes, no other ship would see them, as the Queen had said, until they were up with her and across her rails. He glowed with admiration, for who but Queen Grainne would have thought of this! Now he, Patrick O'Flaherty, too knew the secret of all these daring raids that filled the treasure house of Queen Grainne and left Queen Elizabeth gnawing her nails in fury in the painted rooms of Greenwich Palace, and he drew himself up as tall as all his thin length would allow, his family and his troubles forgotten, stiff with pride and excitement that he was a page to the greatest Queen in Britain.

He had a little trouble with his stomach, unused to the long roll and pitch of the clumsy boat, and a sudden desperate queasiness threatened all his new-found dignity, but he fought it fiercely, gulping at the cold air, and fixing his mind on the high, clear thrum of the wind in the sails. By the time Queen Grainne turned and hissed along the boat that there would now be silence, the sweat along his forehead was cold as the night air itself, and he could not stop the trembling of his braced knees; but he was still standing up, still master of this treacherous, heaving stomach, and still at his post beside his Queen.

He forgot his troubles then in the sudden, hushed excitement that filled the galley as the pinprick lights of the English galleons became clear across the dark sea; sailing lights swaying at their mastheads. There were no more orders, for every man in the boat knew his task exactly at every point, and there was the confidence and subdued hilarity born of many such successful raids on this, their private stretch of sea.

He forgot his duties as a page, too, whatever they might be, and turned his head from side to side as the sails hissed down and the oars thrust out through the holes in the galley sides. They had drawn closer now to the English ship in the center of the three, the warmer lights of her poop deck windows glowing below the masthead lights and showing the faint white shadow of her spreading sails. Near at hand lay the two ships that escorted her, one on each side, but there were no lights to show where Grainne's small fleet slid in silence over the waves that lifted the galleon lights to the black skies and then dropped them again into deep troughs of the sea where they were lost.

"Sea a little heavy, madam," he heard Owen say to the Queen, where she stood wide-legged in the prow of her ship, feet braced to ride the lifting waves.

"It will serve," Grainne answered him. "And serve us better when we are done. There will be storm by morning."

Owen did not reply, and in that moment the sea that had been apparently dark and empty became alive some distance off with the high lights of ships; or so it seemed to the confused and astonished Patch, who had thought the Queen's shallow curraghs to be the only boats abroad besides themselves and the other galley and the English galleons. Now the sea beyond the escort ships was dotted with moving lights, surely too high for these small, flat-bottomed boats? The lights of the escort ships were already swinging towards whatever it was that threatened, and across the water Patch could catch the crack of their turning sails. The ship in the middle came on steadily, her only duty to reach Galway safely with her cargo.

Patch was utterly confused, with no idea what was happening, and the first boom of cannon from the escorting ships made him jump wildly into the air; the dark night was suddenly scarlet with the flash of flame, and the crash echoed like a solid blow across the water as the English fired at the threatening lights that seemed to ring them. One after another the guns roared out, giving the boy for one second a picture of the towering ship, painted in smoking red, marked by the black ugly mouths of her guns, and with the sea heaving underneath her. But there was no answering crash as the balls hit their target; no bursts of flame from the ships that showed the moving lights; only splash after splash into the empty sea, with the sharp smell of gunpowder acrid on the wind. The dark silent boat of Queen Grainne drove steadily ahead as though nothing was happening at all, but beside her, Patch could sense her pleasure and elation that some plan was going exactly as it should.

They were now almost abreast of the center galleon, alone on the sea, and Owen gave one brief order that brought the boat round in a great sweep until Patch was looking up open-mouthed in the darkness at the huge ship that towered above him like a cliff, her guns darker shadows on her sides, and her lights far above him against the night sky. Still no word was spoken.

Every man knew what he must do, and the boy made himself as small as possible in the middle of the sudden hustle of urgent, silent men with coils of long ropes which he had tripped over earlier in the night. Each rope ended in a vicious-looking hook, and the faint thud of them engaging in the carved wood of the poop deck was lost in the receding thunder of the great ships. There were no mistakes, every rope was thrown with the certainty of long practice, and within a few short minutes Patch found himself alone in the prow of the boat, except for a few rowers who remained to hold her in position against the galleon's side. This time Queen Grainne had forgotten him.

He did not know what to do. Not only had she forgotten him, but she had forgotten her cutlass too, the heavy belt still cutting into his shoulder. There was a long time of silence, and he grew desperately anxious that something had gone wrong, but the men seemed unconcerned, whispering quietly together in their moment of peace, expertly keeping their boats from crashing against the bigger ship.

"What of me?" Patch whispered to one of them. "And what of the Queen's cutlass?"

"What of you?" the man said, and the boy caught the gleam of teeth in the blackened face. "And how can the Queen fight without her cutlass? I'd take it after her!"

He was joking, but Patch looked at him, and looked up at the ropes straining up to the galleon's side. It would be easy. There would be footholds in plenty after a few feet on the carved timbers, and she was not nearly as high as she had seemed. It was the sails that made her look so tall and huge. At this moment, pandemonium broke out on the ship above him, and again he caught the satisfied gleam of teeth. There was shouting and the thud of running feet and the occasional dead blast of a blunderbuss; the sudden scream of a wounded man, and above it all the hoarse, cheerful screeching of Grainne, piercing the din with the war cry of the O'Malleys. Patch felt the weight of the cutlass. What was she fighting with? Might she be in danger because she had relied on her page, whatever he was, to follow her? And he had stayed behind. He started up the nearest rope and no one held him back. It was like Clare Island; men's lives were their own, and they did as they would with them.

He got onto the galleon on a narrow, railed gallery some ten feet above the sea, but there was no one there and the sound of fighting was still above him, so he hitched his heavy belt and crept along the planking until, towards the prow of the boat, he found a set of stairs. He could feel that the galleon had come to a halt, and someone up above him was running down the sails, the canvas clattering unfurled to the decks. On the narrow stairs he had to climb around a dead man, an English sailor from the look of his clothes, and when he reached the top, he found he was on some sort of upper deck that looked down into the middle of the ship; and here the fighting was coming to an end.

In the middle of the chaos of unfurled sails and tangled ropes and dead men, the warriors of Queen Grainne had penned the remaining members of the crew into a corner of the deck and, even as Patch came where he could see, a running man extinguished the last light on the galleon so that now she wallowed helpless in a darkness as complete as that of the smaller boats moored against her side. Far away, the escorting vessels still kept up their chase of the elusive lights that had threatened their charge, and down where they could not be seen, a couple of small lanterns guided Grainne in the important work of the night.

She crouched at an open door that led down into the depths of the ship, her crooked, wolfish grin on her face as she watched and counted the coffers and boxes and bales that her men were bringing from the galleon's holds. They worked as always in a silent team; one lot bringing up the goods and passing them to the others, who lowered them carefully over the side to the men waiting in the boats below.

Patch crept a little closer, fascinated, edging down the stairs that led from the high deck down into the center, coming silently behind the Queen as she crouched in the small circle of light. As he reached the ground behind her, he sensed a stir ahead of them, and saw a man raise himself from what had seemed to be a pile of dead. He could not walk, but he was close enough behind the Queen to lift himself on his elbows, grunting with the agony of the last effort he would ever make.

In the lantern light, Patch caught the gleam of the long knife in his hand, inches from the back of the Queen's dark cloak; caught the look of fiendish pleasure on the face of the dying man as he lifted his hand to strike. He knew no thought, nor was there any time to shout. He knew nothing but the sudden feel of the hilt of Grainne's heavy cutlass in his hand, hopelessly heavy; the wild swinging of his body as he struck at the man below him; and the sickening, jarring thud, as the huge cutlass bedded itself in the mast above the Queen's head. The sudden movement had been enough to warn her quick senses; had been too much for the slowing mind of the dying man, halting his hand, and it was the Queen's own knife that killed him as she wheeled like a cat without ever leaving the ground. She did not move even then, crouching there and looking from the shocked and shaking boy to the cutlass bedded in the wood beside her, and the dead man at her feet with the knife still in his hand.

"So, Patrick O'Flaherty," she said, and her eyes glowed at him like coals in the lantern light. "So, you would have killed a man for me, to save me."

Patch nodded, and his eyes now were as sick as his stomach. There had been no time to think that he would kill a man; he had only known his Queen in danger and the cutlass to his hand, and no one nearer than he. It was only fortune that the weapon was so heavy that he had cleaved the mast and not the man, and he knew a weak relief that this was so. But he did not know what to say now, too stunned by the closeness of what he had almost done. Stupidly he held out the scabbard and belt.

"I brought your cutlass, madam," he said, and knew it to be feeble, and could not look at the man who lay between them.

Suddenly the Queen gave her wide, mischievous grin, devilish and endearing.

"I never use the thing, Patrick," she said. "I thought you should have something to carry."

He did not know whether to weep or be furious, and she looked at him again and knew his feelings; the true understanding of Grainne, that bound with love everyone who knew her. Her eyes on him now were dark and sober.

"Whatever the reason I gave it to you," she said, "God knows you did a man's work with it tonight, and if Elizabeth of England has a page like you, Patrick O'Flaherty, then the woman is fortunate. You deserve your name."

She turned away, and Patch swelled and glowed, for he knew she could give him no higher praise, thinking of her young dead husband, who was known as The O'Flaherty of the Wars, chieftain of the fiercest fighting tribe in Ireland. But O'Flaherty or not, he felt suddenly very tired, and could not get away fast enough from the dead man at his feet. The galleon was full of dead men, nor was he any stranger to death, no more than any Irish child of his time, but this man he could not look at, whose death had been almost at his hand. He went quietly back to the gallery where he had come in, and they let him down into the boat as if he were a sack of loot. Dimly he noticed that the sea was dark again and empty, the first faint lightening of dawn creeping into the sky; the water was rougher now, the waves in the failing darkness tipped with foamy crests, and the boats banged and rattled against each other, the men working in a great hurry.

Patch sat himself down in a corner out of the way, and took the belt and scabbard off his shoulder; only then did he remember that he had left the cutlass bedded in the mast. What matter. Sleep was overwhelming. What matter the cutlass or anything else. He was an O'Flaherty worthy of the name; the Queen had said so. He was no longer Patch the dreaming boy, following a few stupid sheep about the mountain. He was a fighting O'Flaherty, page to Grainne, whatever that might be, and one of her men, fighting side by side with her against the English. O'Flaherty! With a sudden shock of memory, he recalled how it was that he had got here, and that his family were paying the price for all his glory in the jail in Newport. But before grief could take him, he was asleep, an O'Flaherty worthy of the name.

It was the motion of the boat that woke him, rising and falling so that he had rolled from where he lay until he was down under the rowers' benches. Stiffly he crept out, sore and wet, for the green seas were pouring over the sides of the boat, rising like walls before they crashed over her in a turmoil of white spray. The morning was of a clear, shining brilliance with the wind screaming in from the ocean, and whirling tattered fragments of black storm cloud across a sky as clean washed as the dawn itself. Patch struggled along to where the Queen stood now in the stern of the boat, looking back across the bay.

To the north, beyond the thrashing turmoil of the water, the great black wall of Achill Head rose like a bastion against the morning sky. Patch grasped the side of the boat and held on, his stomach now mysteriously at ease, but his balance at the mercy of the sea. Grainne turned and looked at him, but did not acknowledge him other than to say, "There she goes! There she goes. Achill will finish the job for me." She grinned with satisfaction, while Patch clung and peered, and through the spray and the piling waves he saw in the end the distant, wallowing hulk of a sailless ship, close in towards the foot of the dreaded cliffs; helpless, with nothing for those on board her but to wait the first rasping jar and the tear of the rocks along her keel, the rending and destruction, the cold, merciless sea.

"No," he cried as when he had watched his family led away. "No, no, no!"

Grainne looked at him in astonishment, and Owen and the other men close by looked as if they thought it time this nonsense with the boy was stopped, and he was kept more in his place. But the Queen did not turn away.

"No what, Patrick O'Flaherty?" She had to shout against the screaming wind.

"She is driving on to Achill Head. And there are men in her?"

"There are indeed, and she will be driftwood in no time at all." Grainne's thin, ugly face was full of satisfaction. "Did we not time it well, Owen and I? And the weather helped us." She stood easily against the buck and tilt of the boat, balanced against the sea she loved, with salt on her lips and the wind in her black hair, whipping it around her face. "A good night's work," she said.

Patch strained to catch a glimpse between the waves of the doomed ship. He had wakened this morning much less of a light-hearted hero; wakened with his mind full of his family and their plight. Already they might even be dead while he was sailing the seas with Queen Grainne. His dream had come true, but in his imagination there had been no family under threat of death, and now, after a night of killing, he was filled only with a confused and desperate feeling that someone must be the first to stop it—to save people like himself and his family, and these sailors drifting to their death for no reason other than that they were unlucky enough to pass within Queen Grainne's reach. He could not even put it into clear thought, but he felt the hopelessness of asking help from Grainne, who thought only of how many English she could kill, and laughed when she made up the reckoning. He was utterly confused. With all his heart he had longed to sail with her and be an outlaw like herself, but he was only twelve and had seen more than his share of destruction and death, and some other part of him craved for safety and his father and mother in peace at their fire, with the little ones about the floor. He was unstrung and frightened by the knowledge of how easily he had almost killed a man himself. Someone must begin to make an end of it.

"Stop it!" he bawled so fiercely and so suddenly that Queen Grainne's eyes left the sea and widened on his face. "Do not let them die!" He staggered close to her, shouting against the thunder of the sea and the whistle and crack of the wind in the sails, grabbing at the Queen herself to stop from falling, or from being swept over the low gunwales.

She caught him and held him at arm's length, her eyes big and derisive and wild.

"Why, why, why!" she shouted at him. "Why should I save these miserable English lives?"

Patch himself could not think why. His head only held this confused certainty that someone must stop, and out of his confusion came his answer, yelled at her through the spray that drenched them both.

"Because . . ." he shouted—and hardly knew what he said—"because of the children in Athenry!"

She was still then, holding him a long moment, with the wind tearing at her wild hair and her dark skirts whipping round her legs. She let Patch go so suddenly that he fell into a swirl of water, and turning to Owen she shouted at him, Owen staring back at her without moving, in stark amazement.

Again she shouted at him and stamped her foot on the wet deck, and Owen turned away then, to cup his hands and roar at the other boat across the gap of tumbling water. Slowly, she drew close and her captain hung across her side to listen. Patch, a little frightened, watched the amazement dawn on his face as he understood what he was told. He looked back at the black wall of Achill Head, and then shrugged and threw out his hands, as if to say, well if it is the Queen's madness, then it is mine also. Slowly against the piling waves, the other boat drew away and turned with flapping, cracking sails, to head back the way that she had come. And now Patch, truly frightened, watched her and wondered at the size of what he had done.

Grainne came back to him, thrusting the wet strands of hair out of her eyes where the salt crusted the long lashes, and glaring at the boy half in exasperation and half in real anger.

"There, O'Flaherty," she shouted, as if she might have been speaking to her own dead Donal. "There! I hope you are well pleased. Now it will be all over Conemara before tomorrow's fires are dead, that Grainne of the Ships has lost the marrow from her bones! She has gone soft, and now takes English prisoners."

Chapter 6

Grainne stood above the piled loot of the galleon in the basement storehouse of her castle, a satisfied grin showing her hooked tooth, and her bright, malicious eyes fixed on her husband across from her in the flickering torchlight.

"Well, Master Burke," she demanded, kicking at an ironbound chest with her bare toes and seeming never to feel the blow. "Tell me now why I should give allegiance to Elizabeth of England! Will I live as well as this, fighting on her side? Will she pay me as well as this? Will she give me, at one swoop, all the gold for Galway?" She cackled triumphantly.

"Will my people live as well as they will live on this?"

Iron Dick looked back at her somberly and sighed. Time was running out. The Lord Deputy of Ireland, Sir Henry Sidney, was already on his progress through the west of Ireland, and due to arrive in Galway at the close of the next week. If he could not bring this proud, willful wife to see reason now, there might never be another chance. He took the last words she said.

"Your people may not live as well, madam, but will the rest of Connaught live at all if you do not agree to serve her? Will they live at all if people like you and John and Ulick of Clanricarde will not agree to let them live? It is you, madam, and such as my lords Ulick and John who are killing the land of Ireland. And no chests of gold are enough to pay for that."

Grainne was getting angry, as always when the unwelcome truth came close to her. Her bare toes were tapping on the damp stones of the floor.

"Stop your preaching, Richard Burke," she said. "When I want a sermon, I can sail to Murrisk for it, and hear it in the Abbey."

She had not answered him, and her irritation showed that she was not indifferent. He watched her, the torchlight gleaming in her long hair and her eyes evasive, for she did not wish to talk more; but he pressed her.

"There is little time, madam. Sir Henry Sidney comes to Galway at the close of next week, to take allegiance from all those who offer it. There will be free pardon for all your crimes . . ."

He had gone too far, and Grainne wheeled on him, her dark face furious.

"My *what!*" she hissed. "I have but kept myself and my people, M'William, and knew only one way to do it!" She grinned, her quick temper ebbing. "Nor am I ashamed of what I do. Elizabeth of England can spare it, nor do I want her pardon. I am a queen myself, and maybe it is I who should pardon her for all the deaths in Ireland!"

"Pardon rather yourself and the Clanricarde brothers, who kill the Irish rather than lose their own power," snapped her husband with sudden and unusual anger, and Grainne looked at him from under her long lashes and did not answer for a moment.

"You are going to Galway yourself next week," she asked meekly, as if she had not heard his last remark.

"I am."

"To offer allegiance and all your lands and men to Elizabeth of England?"

"I will get them back from her in fealty. I had rather hold them that way than lose them altogether, and I wish Ireland free of these bare-shanked Scots who live only on her blood."

Grainne looked at him in surprise, a long look at his flushed face and the unaccustomed heat of his speech, and she ran a finger along the wall beside her, tracing the green dampness of the cracks between the stones. "You care, my Dick," she said in a gentle voice, "about this Ireland?"

Iron Dick was himself again.

"I care, madam," was all he said. "I am the M'William of the Burkes of Mayo. How could I not care, and I charge you to care, too."

She did not seem to have heard him, examining the greened tip of a finger under the torch flare.

"Where will you lodge in Galway?"

"With my cousin, Marcus Burke."

Grainne turned, her eyes bright and frivolous, Ireland apparently forgotten.

"Ah, a grand house! A big, grand house! I will come with you, Richard, for the love of your company for, as you say, they cannot touch me riding into Galway under the mercy of my lord Sidney. I will come with you and show them in their grand houses that a Queen can do as well as they! I will dance a measure and flirt my fan and simper with the best of them. Wait, Richard, you will see!"

She minced across the floor with her shawl drawn tight around her and an imaginary fan flapping in her hand, her bare toes pointed and her yellow skirts swinging, and her husband watched her with anguish on his long face. He had begged her to come, and now that she offered he was in a cold sweat as to what mischief she might make and whom she might insult, riding away with a laugh and a toss of her long hair, never waiting to know what harm she might have done. But he would not stop her; better she should come for mischief than not come at all.

Her dancing came to a halt beside the open door of the warehouse for Owen stood on the steps outside it, a small grin on his face for her nonsense. Owen loved her, and she could never be too foolish for him. Iron Dick loved her too, but she frightened him.

"What is it, Owen?" she asked and dropped her nonsense, and Owen, with a small jerk of his head, indicated that he would rather tell her his news away from Master Burke. Her eyes sharpened at once for she had sent Owen on a special message into Newport, but she just nodded to him and turned back to her husband.

"Well, Richard," she said amiably. "Have you not done admiring the Queen's goods? Better we should lock them up, lest she might come after them!"

Iron Dick moved slowly toward the door.

" We will ride for Galway city together then, madam, in the middle of the week. It is a promise?"

Grainne's eyes were wide and grave.

"A promise, Richard. A promise. I should have myself well settled with my clothes and my fan by then. And shoes, in God's name with heels on them, should I fall flat on my face when I wear them!"

He looked at her, but she looked back with empty, innocent eyes that only blazed into devilment as she turned her back on him to turn with her own hands the big iron key in the door.

"I will go now, and see how these lazy blackguards are tending my ships," she said to him, and Iron Dick bowed his small rigid bow and left her. Grainne looked after him as he climbed the stairs above her at his slow, steady pace, and not even he, with all his knowledge of her, could have read her face. She turned and went out onto the shore, where the first sharp winds of the autumn tore at her hair and set her skirts slapping at her ankles. The sea, under a sky of hazed blue, was as green as the veined marble they took from the hills above Lough Fee, and she stood looking over the great sweep of the bay, and the thousand small green islets that lay between her and the sandhills of the shore; rising above them all was the grape-blue cone of Patrick's mountain with its little coronet of cloud around the peak. She stared at it all and knew the sick lurch of love she always felt for it, this precious piece of Ireland that was all her own, by right of her inheritance and by her own strength and courage, and the fierceness of her own hand. Was she right to hold it for herself alone? Or should she do as her husband said, and think of all Ireland; of a land that could be at peace instead of famished and desolate and starving in the name of freedom; freedom that never seemed to come? The fresh wind teased her hair and blew salt across her face, and she could not think of it all for long. God be thanked, anyway, for Clew Bay, she thought, and the lands and seas of the O'Malleys, and I'll think about the rest of Ireland tomorrow. Tomorrow I will make up my mind!

She went in search of Owen, falling over Patch on the way where he sat on a rock in the sun, fumbling with awkward fingers to twist a piece of rope.

"What, Patrick!" she cried. "Do they make a sailor out of you now? I thought you were my page?"

Patch didn't like to tell her that he had not yet managed to find out what that was, but that the men had told him that if he was going to live on the island, he must learn to make himself useful around a boat or they would throw him in the sea. He was not frightened by their threats, but there didn't seem much to do in this business of being a page, and if he was to be one of the Queen's men, then he must learn to live like one. He stretched his sore, cramped fingers, afraid she would say he should have been running behind her with something, which was all a page seemed to do, but she did not appear to mind, looking, herself, at his raw hands.

"When you're through the skin and down to the bone, it gets a little easier," she said cheerfully and made to pass on.

"Madam," cried Patch desperately, and struggled from the heap of hemp that, harsh and strong-smelling, coiled around his feet. "Madam!"

The Queen stopped, fixing him with flint-gray eyes that dared him to ask what he was going to. His voice faltered and died.

"Well?"

"N-nothing, madam. Nothing."

She glared at him. "You took a lot of trouble climbing out of that rope nest to tell me nothing or to ask me nothing! Climb back in now, my fledging, and stay where you belong!" At the last moment before she walked away, she turned again. "Did I not tell you to trust me," she said fiercely, and left Patch behind her, gazing after her with an excited grin, his feet deep in the flaxen hemp and his own length of forgotten rope unraveling in his hand.

"Owen!" bawled Queen Grainne, when she saw him working in one of the curraghs. "Owen!"

Owen came, pushing up his tangle of black curls from his forehead, and saying what he had to say before anyone else might come.

"I did as you bid, madam, riding into Newport last night. I took this jail guard who is my far kin into a tavern and plied him well with ale. But the birds have flown."

"What mean you?" Grainne looked at him in sharp dismay, shocked at the strength of her anxiety that she might not help that skinny little towhead to get his family back. "What mean you, *flown*?"

"With the Lord Deputy coming to the City next week, madam, the English have of a sudden got very troubled about everybody having a fair, public trial."

Grainne snorted.

"There is always time for change," she said derisively.

"So," Owen went on, "all the prisoners in these local jails are being taken into Galway for trial next week, so that if my lord Sidney takes it in mind to visit the courts on any day, then he'll find the fairest of English justice being meted out to the most humble of the Irish."

Grainne made no comment.

"Galway jail," she said thoughtfully. "That'll be by the East

Gate?"

Owen nodded.

"I'd rather be sure of it," Grainne went on, "and not risk waiting for English justice, however fair for my lord Sidney. There'd be no chance of taking them on the way from Newport to Galway city?"

Owen shook his head doubtfully.

"There will be many more besides the ones we want," he said, "and we'd find it hard to separate them. There'll be a heavy guard, too. No, madam, secretly from Galway jail is the only way."

"It is, too, and very secretly," his Queen answered with a wry grin. "For Master Burke rides to Galway to meet my lord Sidney, weighed down with honor and righteousness to protest his loyalty. So whatever we do, Owen, must be done in utter secrecy, for we cannot have Master Burke's lady wife fighting the English in the streets of Galway this week, above all weeks."

"No, madam," Owen said, and his grin was as wide as her own. Grainne tapped her teeth thoughtfully.

"A list, Owen," she said. "We must have a list of every guard in Galway jail. There must be some O'Malley or O'Flaherty who would be willing to stretch a hand to help his kin. Especially for a fistful of gold. Now get to your own work—you have plenty of good help."

She gestured sardonically at the English prisoners from the galleon, who worked in apparent content beside the Irish on the boats.

"There's no harm in them," Owen answered. "And I'd not mind them beside me on a raid. And they think well of you, madam, that they are not shut in some dark cell below the sea."

The Queen shrugged.

"I think so much of cells myself," she said, "that I would rather die at the bottom of the sea or anywhere else than face one. That is why I never took a prisoner. I thought they would rather die, too."

Owen left her and she went thoughtfully back toward the castle, where she must talk with Honor on this matter of suitable finery and shoes with heels on if they killed her. She would not have all these grand Burkes in Galway city looking down their long, sad noses at her in old skin shoes. Thinking this she suddenly sniffed and grinned. Shoes or not, there'd be none of these women could take a galleon like she took that one three nights back! Her face sobered again then and her eyes fell from the sunlit flanks of the far mountains to rest thoughtfully on the rocks at her feet, for this boy O'Flaherty and his family were an embarrassment, and that was the truth, at this very moment when Richard was set on being so loyal and virtuous.

He was her husband and, however she might tease him, once they were away from Clare Island and the secrecy of the sea, she would make no trouble that might harm him at this time. The O'Flahertys were a matter for a dark night and no names known, and the devil himself knew how she was going to manage that in the circumstances.

In the days that followed, she would not yield an inch to her husband, insisting, while she pranced up and down her chamber in bright lengths of wool long stored in musk, that she only went to Galway with him for the company, and for want of entertainment. Honor sewed away desperately by the fire, and in between her prancings, Grainne sat before a mirror trying on every ornament and jewel that had graced the gentler ladies of the O'Malley family.

"Richard!" she said to him, grinning across the room from

under a small pointed coronet of gold, dropped rakishly onto her uncombed hair. "Have I not sent a man hard riding into Galway ahead of me to see about these shoes with heels on, so set am I to be a lady for these Burkes of yours! Here, Patrick—polish this one!" Patch had to jump to catch the coronet as it came flying across the room, for Grainne had suddenly remembered again that she should have a page, and he had been dragged from his happy occupations with the men to help her polish all the gold and trinkets and to be measured like herself for bright new clothes, for her page, too, must be a credit to Richard Burke in Galway.

"I'll warrant none of these Burke women have a page," she said triumphantly, and Patch looked at her, apparently buried in all this foolery, and not for the first time he wondered if he was mad to trust her. Was his family already dead in Newport jail while Queen Grainne breathed on ancient pieces of gold, and jested about her shoes and his own new-cut hair?

Richard Burke tried still to make her see that there were more important reasons for going to Galway.

"Madam, Connaught is wild with rumor, and the list of Irish chiefs who are going to surrender to the Lord Deputy is as long as the waters of Lake Shindilla." He named a lake that ran for nine miles through the mountains of his territory.

Grainne snorted. "Even Shindilla comes at last to its end," she said.

"The list of those who will surrender does not end without the names of John and Ulick of Clanricarde," he said, and watched to see this major thrust go home.

"I do not believe it," said Queen Grainne flatly, but her hands grew still on the braids she plaited for a girdle. Patch looked from one to the other at the mention of my lords John and Ulick, his mind on Athenry and on the astonishing moment when he had bawled at the Queen on the boat the other morning and she had done as he had bidden. She had never spoken of it since. There might indeed be peace in Connaught if the proud Clanricarde brothers came to heel, and someone has to stop it first, he thought as he had earlier on the boat. He waited anxiously for the rest of the conversation.

But Grainne only tossed her head.

"They are but the sons of an Earl," she said, "and not a Queen as I. They have not so much to lose." Her face set into obstinate lines, and her husband sighed and left her to her finery. But Grainne looked after him with all obstinacy gone. Ulick and John! If they were indeed to line up with Elizabeth, then the core of all rebellion would be gone from Connaught, and she might as well lay up her ships and take to being the lady wife of Richard Burke of Burrishoole, and that was no task for her. In a moment she brightened, for were there not still the Spanish! It might be she could make a living from the Spanish ships, and surely her sister Queen would be grateful for the harassing of Spain, although there would be small entertainment in harassing them just to please someone else! She was Grainne of the Isles, and wanted to answer to no one but herself. But what of Ireland, if John and Ulick were giving in for Ireland's sake? She turned a huge enameled brooch between her fingers and her black brows closed down above her eyes. Then Honor came to show her a new gown of saffron silk, just finished, and Grainne tossed aside her cares, holding up the gown and smoothing the lovely folds in the candlelight. Tomorrow she must be ready to go to Galway, and after that she would decide about Ireland and what she would do. Afterwards.

Patch found it hard not to be a little frightened when, some days later, he found himself in the streets of Westport, feeling the eyes of every English soldier on him as if they knew him for who he was. Their eyes were in truth on Queen Grainne O'Malley, as were the eyes of all the people from the country around who had gathered to watch her riding off to Galway. Patch would have been a very small prisoner compared to her, an outlaw declared, like the Clanricarde brothers, with five hundred English crowns upon her head. But all the Irish riding into Galway city were under pardon and protection of Sir Henry Sidney, who was gaining more peace in Ireland by reason and justice than had ever been gained there by the sword. It was in any case a small army few would have cared to hinder that set out southwards, for the train of O'Malleys and O'Flahertys that had disembarked from Clare Island was joined at Newport by the following of Burkes from the lands of Iron Dick at Burrishoole. Led by Grainne in a scarlet cloak with her husband dark and somber at her side, they left the sunset flaming behind them over Clew Bay, and faced down the lonely track across the bog, watched by the distant mountains, where Patch had first encountered the Queen; they headed down for Ballinrobe and Headford and, in the blue early morning, the hospitable Abbey of Annaghdown. Here the vast company heard Mass above the glittering waters of Lough Corrib and broke their fast, before they faced the last long stretch straight without a bend into the heart of Galway city.

Chapter 7

All Connaught seemed to have gathered into the gray City of the Tribes for the visit of the Lord Deputy, thronging the narrow streets and filling the houses; wild with talk and rumor as to what his presence might bring. In the first hour of dusk, it was a dazed and bewildered Patch who was at last allowed to escape from the dark paneled parlor of Marcus Burke. There, for hours, he had shifted from foot to foot in his uncomfortable shoes, standing behind his Queen as she made bored and condescending conversation with the ladies of the great house and their other guests. The city had confused him from the first, so large and crowded, sprawling its high gray walls along the banks of the Corrib where it tumbled into the sea, with all the narrow streets close lined with these tall stone houses that shut out the light from the sky, every one of them almost as big as the keep of the island castle itself.

When he was at last allowed to go, he had difficulty finding his way through the maze of passages and paneled galleries down to the kitchens, and out across the torchlit yard to the huge stable block where Queen Grainne's men were quartered.

"Ah, towhead," said one of them, turning from the care of his tired horse. "What think you of the fine life in there?" He peered at him in the warm flicker of light and laughed. "You do not look as if it suits you much!"

"I'faith," said Patch, "I'd be better off on Clare Island."

"Who wouldn't?" answered the man. "Who wouldn't?"

Patch eased the shoes from his aching feet and looked around the high-walled yard. His Queen had said, somewhat to his surprise, that she would not need him again that evening. She had been so proud of him, for no lady of the Burkes had thought to have a page, and the whole afternoon it had been Patrick come here, and Patrick give me that, and Patrick get me this, until his feet ached and his head grew dazed with sleepiness from the long night's riding. He was oppressed by the hot smell of the tiered candles that blazed along the walls and the heavy perfume of the ladies' clothes, while his hungry stomach nagged him with the sight of the good dinner on the table under his eyes. There was cold food now laid out for the men in the middle of the yard, and he fell on it without asking, remembering his first lessons in the island castle in the matter of caring for himself.

He did not know where to sleep, and he asked the men who had spoken to him when he came in. He looked at him and said, "Where you fall, towhead, and that will likely be soon enough." There was too much noise in the vast, raftered stables where the men lay in the straw, drinking ale and throwing dice, their long ride done and their horses safely bedded, and their Queen for the moment well watched over by her hosts. Patch wandered across the yard, drowsy to the point of falling, looking only for a soft spot as the man had said. He found it in the far shadows of the yard, beyond the torchlight and the noisy stables, where there was an angle in the wall and a pile of sacks close beside a small door. The sacks were soft and hairy underneath his face; warm and easy; welcoming.

He had no idea what time it was when he started violently awake, dizzy and confused from the heavy depth of his sleep, blinking around at the night sky dark as pitch, and the small gleam of lantern light from the now silent stables. The big house that had earlier blazed with light from all its windows was now no more than a vast shadowy bulk of darkness against which he could see nothing, but he knew for certain that what had awakened him was the shutting of the door behind his head. Who could have been going out thus secretly in the dark hours of the night, for the chill and silence of the curfewed streets beyond the walls told him it was very late. It took but a few moments to shake himself awake and climb out of his sacks to follow, forgetting all about his shoes; but the pitch darkness when he himself opened the gate told him nothing other than that he was in some narrow passage between high stone walls, their chill close by him on both sides.

He was about to turn away, when from somewhere along to his right, he heard a sudden burst of laughter, quickly stifled, and knew it at once for what it was. What was Queen Grainne doing, wild though she might be, creeping in the night from the house of her husband's kinsman? What mischief was she up to now? In the darkness he grinned, for the short time he had been her page had taught him that where his mistress was, then there was usually trouble of some kind, too, and often she was the only one who found it funny. After one cautious glance back, he slipped out into the narrow lane, game for whatever was afoot.

It was possible to touch both walls by holding out his hands, and he made good speed until the lane branched, and there he came to a helpless halt. There was no sound in the night save for an owl hooting softly somewhere in the garden, and the cold slap of the sea against stone, which told him he must be close beside the river walls. The smell of salt water was sharp on the cool air. Faintly, away to his left, he thought he heard the small chink of a sword, and then the voice of a night watchman drowned it, crying four of the clock, somewhere toward the middle of the town. Hopefully, Patch turned and followed where he thought he had heard the chink of arms.

In a moment he found himself out in the open streets, the cobbles painful to his bare feet and the tall stone houses rearing above him in the darkness, patched here and there even now, with squares of candlelight, as if those who gathered to settle the fate of Ireland could waste no time in sleeping. Here there was danger of being caught by the watch, or by the bands of soldiers who were moving night and day through the city, with the person of Sir Henry Sidney in their care. He almost turned back, but felt himself drawn on by the sense of someone always just ahead of him, where he could not see. Blindly he followed, and by now he wondered why he did. If it were Queen Grainne, then she might not thank him, for if she had wanted him, would she not have told him to come? With some dogged obstinacy he pressed on, and quite soon he knew himself to be alone, with no sight or sound of anyone around him, and completely lost. He seemed to be in a large square of open space, and when he stumbled over the edges of some steps, he looked up a moment at the shadowy cross that reared above them, and then sat down patiently below it to wait for light. He told himself he had nothing to fear. He had a right to be in the city, and was here under the protection of his Queen. But what right had he, a felon in the English eyes, to be abroad before dawn with no reason to give for it if he was asked. He shivered and drew his knees up to his chin, the darkness suddenly more threatening, and he huddled down as small as possible on the steps while his ears strained for the slightest noise. If he could dodge the watch until the dawn, then the streets would be full again and he could mingle with the crowds and find his way back to the house of Marcus Burke. He prayed a little, and thought of his family in Newport jail, and prayed for them too, and waited and watched for the sky to lighten above the gabled roofs.

Down by the East Gate, Grainne had calculated the darkness to a nicety. For many days she had had a man watching the habits and routines of the men on guard at the high gates of the jail, but she had found neither O'Malley nor O'Flaherty, who might help their tribe for gold.

"It rests with me then, Owen," she had said, and Owen nodded, with a little less than his usual confidence. This was a doubtful business, under the nose of the Lord Deputy himself, and it was possible that even the long-faced husband of the Queen might be tried too far. But he knew better than to argue with his mistress.

"You have chosen my man carefully?" she asked him, and he nodded.

"Ah yes, a soft fellow no good for anything but to hold a key and turn it, and weep then for those he locks up!" Owen snorted. "But there he is and on duty in the dark hours tonight. It is tonight or not at all, madam." Now it was tonight, and with Owen and half a dozen chosen men, she lay back in the darkest shadows near the main gate of the jail.

"Are you ready, Owen? You all know what to do?"

Owen whispered, "Yes, madam," and she sensed the others nodding in the darkness. She gave a small laugh of pure excitement, such as Patch had caught from her as she left the back gate of the yard; this was a revel after her own heart, and if all went well, the O'Flaherties would be safe away before the dawn, and none to miss them till the morning meal, such as it was— God help them all in there. Owen would go in and call them out, and who would know in the darkness of that place that he was not what he seemed.

A few moments later, the guard at the outer gate of the jail heard a small whimper, as of a woman in distress, and the soft-hearted fellow, so carefully chosen, came forward from his small tower and peered through the spy hole of his great gate. He could see her clearly, the poor creature, bent double with some agony, dragging herself along and moaning pitifully.

"What is it, ma'am? What ails you?" he asked through the opening, and got no answer, and doubtfully he peered back across the drawbridge to the main gate where his sergeant was. Surely there was no danger at this time of night, with all the vagabonds locked up tightly for the night, and the poor creature moaning there like death itself. When she slipped to the ground just beyond his gate, he did not hesitate any more, but turned his key in the postern gate with his eyes on the poor soul moaning with even greater agony, whatever was wrong with her. He did not even take his key, but left it in the postern lock as he hurried over to her.

It was Owen's arm that took him around the throat, and he never reached the poor moaning woman, who leaped to her feet with her grinning teeth white in the darkness and beckoned to the men behind her in the shadows as the body of the guard slid over the bridge and the water closed above it.

"Now the next one," hissed Grainne, and this had to be done by surprise; there were a sergeant and two men in the guard room at the other end of the drawbridge. In bare, silent feet they whipped across the bridge, the three men snoozing by a brazier at the other end, with the calm certainty of the outer guard to raise an alarm before anything could reach them from beyond the walls. In a few moments, Grainne would have the keys, and there were ways of making these fellows tell them where the O'Flahertys lay.

The Governor of the jail had dined that night with all the gorgeous company who waited on my lord Sidney. He was an aging man whose stomach had long lost its pleasure in rich foods and too many wines and, like Patch, he was waiting wearily for the dawn after a long, sleepless night. In his restless walking, he reached his casement just as the shadow of Grainne and her men swept over the bridge below him, dark against the pale planks, and his indigestion had done nothing to cloud his mind. Even as the sergeant fell to Grainne's knife, and her fingers fumbled at the chain of keys, the Governor reached down his horn, and away at the Market Cross, Patch had heard the long, winding note and started up, certain of danger.

He heard confused shouting in the distance, growing closer, and he stood below the cross peering into the darkness, wild with anxiety, for some certain instinct told him that the center of the trouble would be Queen Grainne. Hesitantly, he ran forward in the darkness towards the sound of shouting, and now the clash of swords and running footsteps. There were more shouts too, coming from other directions, as though the town woke and the Watch was alerted; soon the streets would be full of danger and, without being told, Patch knew that this danger would be for his Queen. Frantically he searched the night, guided only by the noise, which was now confused so that he had no idea where it came from. One lot of running steps seemed to separate from the others and to grow closer, then out of one of the side streets two figures ran, clinging to each other, stumbling along as best they could, one with a long cloak and the other with the gleam of a naked sword in his hand.

Patch ran forward as the cloaked figure fell and the man did his best to hold her up. Light was growing with every second, and Owen, his face smeared with blood, looked at Patch with gratified astonishment.

"Care for her, boy," he said. "Get her home. I must get back to the others at the jail."

Then he was gone, running back as fast as he had come to where his men still needed him, wherever that might be, and Patch had all the weight of Queen Grainne around his neck; he could feel his face already wet like Owen's with the blood flowing from a wound in her shoulder. She seemed to realize that it was only the boy and made a great effort to straighten up and take her weight from him.

"Just give me a shoulder, Patrick. Just a shoulder and I will walk. Get us home now, in God's name, or my husband will be lost with my lord Sidney. No use for him to make peace with his wife raiding the streets of Galway in the dark!" She tried to laugh and gasped a little, and Patch felt her become heavier.

"Do not speak, madam," he said, and had little breath to do it himself, with all his mind bent on praying to God to show him the way to go. It would indeed be in God's name if they got home at all. The day was growing lighter, and he did his best to remember the turnings he had taken, looking with amazement and relief at the door in the wall that he recognized only by the curious handle he had felt beneath his hands in the night. Grainne, white as a waxen candle in the dawn light, lifted her eyes to the Burke arms carved in stone above the door, and with an effort she turned and smiled at him.

"God was with us, Patrick," she said faintly, "even though we were up to such evil."

He did not ask her how she would fare inside—it was more than he could face to tackle the burden of getting her through the house and she seemed quite content that she should be left within the kitchen door. He nearly wept with sheer relief when in the gray stone passage, Honor came silently from the shadows, with one sweeping glance across the blood and the white face of her mistress. Without a word she took the sagging weight of Grainne, and gestured the boy outside with a sharp motion of her head. Sweating, Patch closed the door behind him, his mind now on Owen and the others in the growing day, and quickly he went back across the pard to the pump, to try and wash the dark, spreading blood from his new clothes before the first restless stirrings of men and horses in the stables; and to find his new shoes where he had forgotten them, on the heap of sacks beside the door.

It was not long before Owen came back, and with him only three men. He turned a firm, quieting gaze on Patch that forbade the boy ask a question; and the men now up and moving around the yard, looked at the blood on the clothes of Owen and the other three, and carefully busied themselves about their horses, and seemed to notice nothing. It was as if the three men who did not break their fast that morning, had never been among the others, and Patch thought of his first day on Clare Island, where he had come a stranger, and no one had asked a question. So it seemed, in this company, you could go too, forever, and no one would ask where or why.

It was not until evening that Patch was summoned to his Queen, and he had had a long day for thinking, all his thoughts revolving around the words that Owen had flung at him as he gave him the wounded Queen.

"I must go back to the others at the jail."

It was possible that there were other reasons why Grainne should try to raid a jail at this moment when it was vital that the English should think well of her husband. But Patch could think of only one reason why she should do so, and he was sick with gratitude that she would risk all for him.

In the small private parlor which the Burkes had given her, she was sitting up very straight beside the fire, her left arm quiet across her lap and her proud face looking pale and shadowed under her black hair. She looked at him grimly, and there was no one else in the room.

"Well, O'Flaherty," she said, and again it was as if she spoke to her dead Donal. "We have a secret, you and I. You will keep it?"

Patch did not even bother to answer that.

"Madam," he said urgently. "You did this for me. You did

this to save my family. You tried to get them."

Immediately she looked furious, her strained white face creasing with irritation.

"What business is it of yours, Patrick O'Flaherty," she demanded, "what I was doing? Did I not tell you to mind your own business?"

This time Patch did not flinch and run, but grinned at her, and slowly she grinned back at him.

"What if I did?" she said, as if she were a child caught in mischief. Then her face sobered, and she suddenly looked ill and very tired. "But I'll tell you something, Patrick. We haven't got them yet." Her face grew distant. "I am not sure," she said musingly, "but that your family and Ireland may not prove to be one and the same thing. I think that is what my long-faced Richard meant."

Patch looked at her, so unnaturally quiet and weary, and would have given his life for her; but he did not understand what she had said.

Chapter 8

The following day was Sunday, a fair September day of high idling clouds across a clear blue sky, with Galway Bay lying smooth as silk and the hills of Clare dreaming in their haze beyond it. In the soft sunshine, the people of the city came crowding early into the streets, for the Lord Deputy was to attend the morning service at the Parish Church of St. Peter, with all the high Anglo-Norman families joining him to show their respect for him and their loyalty to the Queen of England. While the day was still young, and the mist not yet cleared from the silken sea, the streets were loud with the noise of the chattering, jostling throng, humming with talk and speculation as to which of the Irish chiefs might be joining in this church parade, word running from mouth to mouth as to those of them who had already been seen in the city.

Queen Grainne was not so anxious to go out. In her dark, paneled room she sat obstinately in bed, holding her left arm tight against her and glaring mulishly at her husband. Iron Dick stood at the foot of the bed, one hand spread to each of the carved oaken posts, and looked at her beseechingly.

"I beg you, Grainne," he said, "and it is not much for you to do."

Grainne's long mouth twitched defiantly.

"This St. Peter's is not my church, nor is it yours either, Richard Burke, and we have no cause to go there. I will hear my Mass where I can with my own people, and my lord Sidney may say his prayers for himself, for marry, in this town I think he needs them. He knows not who is for him or against him, or whose sword may take his ribs if he fail to look around fast enough."

Iron Dick urged her.

"Then, madam, admire him for his courage, thus to show himself so publicly, for courage is a thing you value. We could show him who is with him, and then the people of the city will know too, and feel more settled to see their chiefs seeking to make peace for them."

"Then do you go yourself, since you are so heart set on peace with my enemies!"

"They do not seek to be your enemies, if you will be their friend."

Grainne snorted, and winced as the small movement jagged her wound.

"What ails you?" her husband asked, and for a moment she felt tempted to use her wound as an excuse, making up some story as to how she got it. Then she straightened, shocked that she, Grainne O'Malley, should seek excuses for anything that she did. Grainne O'Malley did as she thought fit, and did not offer explanation or excuse to any man.

"Remember," Iron Dick went on, never waiting for her answer, "you mean more to these people here than any other chief. They will be watching for you, led by what you do today. Think of Ireland, madam! Think of Ireland!"

Grainne leveled her gaze at him through slits of eyes as gray as slate.

"I do not need you, M'William Eughter, to tell me what to do about my people. And I told you that I came here only to bear you company. I made no promise for your Henry Sidney."

Baffled, Richard turned away, and behind his back, the angry face softened into a grin of mischievous affection and then sobered again. What indeed was she to do both for Ireland and for herself; not forgetting these miserable O'Flahertys that she had failed to snatch from jail. A *pest* on all O'Flahertys! They were more trouble to her than all Ireland, and never before had a prank so bothered her conscience. A pest on this boy Patrick, too, coming to Clare Island and fixing her with these great accusing eyes, and then, perdition take him, trusting her that she could do everything to save his family. Why did people have to look at her as if they *trusted* her, the boy O'Flaherty, and that big, long, foolish husband of hers, gazing at her with his sheep's eyes and waiting for her to do the right thing. And what indeed, she must decide, was the right thing, for her, for Ireland, and for Patrick O'Flaherty and all his family. Cautiously she stretched and peered through the small panes of her casement at the bright skies of the young day, and caught the hum and mutter of the streets outside. It was a grand day, she realized, and high time that she was up and doing in it. Soon, soon, she would decide about Ireland, but now for the moment she was hungry. She pulled herself up as best she could on one arm, and bawled for Honor to come and see her dressed, putting Ireland from her mind until later.

Close to noon, the company that was to ride to St. Peter's Church gathered in the hall in the house of Marcus Burke, with the sun streaming in the tall windows to fall in golden pools across their feet, catching the sheen of satin and the soft gleam of velvet from their clothes; lighting the high, lovely colors of flowing skirts, and the gold and silver of embroidered doublets; gleaming white on the crisped edges of laced ruffs and winking in the jewels of necklaces and sword hilts. They moved proudly, these Burkes, in their bright colors and their jewels, certain of themselves, the loyal ones, the salt and nobility of the City of Galway, on whom Sir Henry Sidney could only look with favor. They were sure of their position and of their superiority to these warring Irish riding in from their savage country castles, to fill the streets with their wild followers and their uncouth language. They looked with kindness at their cousin Richard, who had ridden in from Mayo to make it quite clear that he was one of them, and the ladies listened with smirking condescension to the excuses he made for his wife, this so-called Queen, that she did not seem well enough to ride with them to church.

"Queen Grainne indeed," whispered Amelia Burke to her daughter, as well as she could whisper in the foot-high ruff that would not let her bend her head. "Queen of the Savages, I would say, and we are far better off without her, for she would surely do some outrageous thing to shame us."

Her daughter nodded, for her ruff was smaller and let her

show her feelings just a little. They had all suffered much in these last days from the crude and hurtful directness of Grainne, who would have none of their grand airs and formal ways, belittling them with wide, derisive eyes even when she said nothing, and shocking everyone with her rough, outlandish manners. And the ugliness of the woman!

Everything was ready and it was time for them to go. The big oaken door stood open to the sunshine and in the paved court beyond the grooms were waiting with the horses in the gentle jingle of harness and the soft clop of a restless hoof, while the disturbed doves cooed and circled over their heads. Marcus Burke offered his arm to his wife, Amelia. In his finery he was a splendid figure, as tall as his cousin Richard of Mayo, but heavier; formal and magnificent today in a velvet suit the color of the leaves of autumn, laced with silver and with silver embroidery the long length of his silken hose. Behind him, Richard, more sober in his usual black, moved sadly to take the arm of the daughter of the house, in the absence of Grainne. As he bowed and reached out his hand, he was halted by a sharp voice from the stairs behind him, cutting like a knife across the urbane murmurs of the Burkes.

"So, Richard Burke, you leave your wife to ride alone! It does not matter, for a Queen needs none to ride with her."

They all wheeled where they stood, and there was no sound save the soft noises of the courtyard, the waves of surprise and jealousy filling the bright hall like the dark clouds of a coming storm. And she held them there, coming down the stairs slowly, a little stiffly, but with all the fierce pride and dignity of the generations of proud O'Malleys who had gone to make her what she was. Against the brilliant color of the silks and velvets and glittering jewels, she was dressed with utter plainness in the fine wools woven by the people of her island kingdom; a swirling kirtle of ancient saffron yellow like the warriors of old, and a white cloak held across her breast by a great gold broach as pale as the color of her skirt. Her bare feet were thrust into soft skin shoes sewn for her by the fisherfolk of her seashores, whispering down the stairs as softly as if she wore no shoes at all, and her proud black head was bare, crowned only by the piled masses of her black hair, brushed and gleaming from Honor's loving hands. She looked as royal as the Hill of Tara, and as proudly Irish as the gray stones of her mountains, but while her dark, ugly face was composed in severe and determined dignity, she could not prevent the bright eyes from snapping with satisfaction back and forth across the startled, jealous faces of the gathered company. Behind her walked Patch, hastily summoned from the stable yard to be resentfully washed and brushed by Honor, carrying in his hand his Queen's Missal, for she would not go, she said, into some heathen church without the word of God in her hand. His clean face shone with all his pride that she could indeed fulfill his dreams by looking so much a Queen and, for the moment, he had forgotten all about his family. It was enough to walk behind his Queen.

At the bottom of the stairs, Richard Burke moved away from his outraged niece, and there was an expression on his face in which pride and tenderness and wild exasperation were well mixed, as he gave his hand to his unpredictable wife. She forgot her dignity and gave him a broad malicious grin.

"Do not count on anything, my Dick," she said. "I told you I came only to bear you company." Her eyes flashed derisively around the resentful ladies in their peacock finery, who had dismissed her as an island savage not worthy of their notice. "And I could not help, husband," she added, "but put these ruffled hens where they belonged!"

Put them where they belonged she did, for on the ride through the city to where St. Peter's stood upon its hill, no one in the packed streets had eyes for other than Queen Grainne. The people ran at her stirrup, bringing her horse almost to a halt, wild with pride in her that she was so arrogantly Irish in the midst of this fine cavalcade of Anglo-Normans. They cried to her for themselves and held up their children for them to see her; running beside her to beg her in the name of Ireland to find peace in some way for them and for their families. At her side, Richard Burke rode with hooded eyes and said nothing, watching the sadness of her troubled face as she listened and nodded to them, and eased the clutching hands from her yellow skirts. And behind her rode Patch, sitting his pony more easily now, as he listened too, and wanted to cry aloud to them that of course she would do what was best for Ireland. How could she not, who had been willing to do so much for his family who were nothing to her? He had begun to understand the strong and tender character that lay under the wildness of his capricious Queen Grainne, and he wanted to shout out and assure these clamoring people that if they were in her hands, then they were safe. She would laugh at them and tease them till she drove them mad; she would demand their love and service to death itself, but she would never fail to care for them. These things he had learned in his short time in the gray, sea-washed walls of the castle at Clare Island.

When at last they reached it, the gray church was already crowded, but place had been kept for the great ones like the Burkes, and with them Grainne was led to the very front, looking around her with unhidden astonishment at the talking, excited crowd of fashionable people.

"I'faith Dick," she said, hitching at her saffron skirts and enjoying to the full the curious glances that followed her up the aisle. " 'Tis more like a gathering for a dancing or a cock fight, than a crowd of people come to say their prayers!"

Patch remained at the back with the other servants, squeezed into a corner immediately inside the porch door of the church, so that he had a clear view both up the long nave and down the steps outside; over the sloping square where the crowds now waited in silence for the coming of Sir Henry Sidney. He came last of all, when the church was full, a slender man and not very tall with a high forehead above his thin, intelligent face, and a small fair beard. Up the last slope to the steps of the church he rode in a silence as deep and complete as night across the bogland, the eyes of every person fixed on him, and the noise of hooves as loud as thunder in the uncanny hush. All around him were soldiers, their armor gleaming in the soft sun and light pricking from the tips of their lances, but at the bottom of the steps he waved them all away. Alone, he walked steadily into the church, a quiet figure placing his unhurried feet firmly on the long flight of steps; wearing a plain suit of dark brown velvet with a long gold chain about his neck. If his mind in that moment dwelt on the thrown spear that might take him helpless in the back, his tranquil face showed nothing of his thoughts. Patch in his corner, so close that he could have touched him, looked up into the dignified face with its quiet half-smile, and sensed at once that here was another strength as firm and dependable as that of his wild Queen. He felt all at once safe, and wildly excited. Someone, he had shouted that morning in the boat, had got to stop it all! *Was* this the man who might do so? Was this calm, fragile-looking man the one who might bring peace to Ireland, and let them all grow up without fear?

For a long time he had no eyes for anyone save the Lord Deputy, craning to watch all he could see of his fair head up at the far front of the church, bent respectfully for the prayers of the Archbishop of Galway that murmured through the gray stones above the bowed forest of plumes and velvet. The new noise that was filling the streets had grown loud and close before he noticed it and turned his head, suddenly aware of uproar and commotion far down the hill, in the crowd that had been still and quiet as the congregation in the church. People were running up the long slope that led down to the water, breaking the lines in which they stood along the sides of it; grasping anyone they could and shouting at them; and even in the distance the boy could sense the amazement and fear that was running through the people like wind across a summer sea. Down below in the square, women heard the running whispers and shrieked and clasped their children, but in the tight-packed crowd there was no place for them to run. Men shouted and jostled, and all eyes were turned toward the far end of the square, from where the uproar could be heard swelling and approaching through the streets. From the steps of the church, outraged officials sent soldiers flying to suppress the noise, and armor flashed in the sun as horses wheeled and pushed, but the crowd looked at them as if they were not there, and still talked and craned and jostled, climbing on each other's backs to get a better view.

In the end it was all for one young man who rode alone, bareback on a hungry-looking horse and, as he came clearly into the square, a silence fell again with a hush far more deadly than had fallen even for Sir Henry Sidney; a hush that was a drawn breath of pity and admiration, and with them the cold breath of a long-known terror. As the man drew closer, Patch could see he looked as hungry as his horse, a great gaunt giant, with his black hair cropped to tell the world he was Irish and his saffron kilt tattered and shabby around his knees. His woolen cloak was threadbare and his skin shoes broken, but his head was in the air, great arrogant nose defying pity and eyes blazing from under heavy brows as though daring anyone to stop him and ask him what he did. No man moved to do so, but the whisper ran before him through the crowd, and even the English soldiers stopped in their tracks and stared at him, and looked bewildered at their officers as if to ask them what to do.

"Ulick of Clanricarde!" The shocked murmur ran among the crowd. "It is the lord Ulick, come in to surrender!"

No one interfered, for no one seemed to know what they should do, and in silence with no man near him, Ulick of Clanricarde, the most terrible rebel in all of Connaught, drew his horse to stand at the foot of the church steps; and swinging down he left it there, its thin head drooping and the reins trailing to the ground. As he walked up the steps, firm and deliberate as my lord Sidney, he drew his long sword slowly from its scabbard, which was still the one rich and splendid thing about him, and a great gasp went up, for who knew what he meant to do. One imperious gesture waved back the officers who stepped forward, and Ulick of Clanricarde moved on into the church. His passage up the long aisle stilled the prayers and lifted breathless faces until he stood at the foot of the steps below the altar, where the Archbishop had already turned to face him after one anxious glance at Sir Henry Sidney, who had not moved beyond to lift his head. The Archbishop, gazing at him sternly from the altar, showed no fear of the giant with the naked sword, but from his place of honor near the Lord Deputy, the old Earl of Clanricarde rose slowly to his feet, his face working as he stared at his eldest son.

"And what do you do here?" the Archbishop asked the young man coldly. "What do you do here, Ulick de Burghe, coming with your bare sword into the house of God?"

The answer was barely audible, as though the young man was very tired, but the gray eyes fixed the priest as sternly as his own, and the proud head never dropped.

"I am here in peace, my lord Archbishop, and come to surrender my sword on your altar for the sake of Ireland. And for her sake I will treat with those that wish to speak with me."

The Archbishop moved forward to take the sword, and it was as though the whole silent church sighed at the weight of death it carried, and what it might mean for troubled Connaught if it could be sheathed forever. Even as he turned and laid it on the altar, the murmuring was swelling again in the crowd outside, and another young man came up the steps to walk the length of the wide sunlit aisle; as large and thin and shabby as the first one, but as fair as he was dark, younger, with his cropped hair curling around a face belonging to a youth not far from boyhood. The sword he handed to the Archbishop was heavy with the same weight of blood and death, and the old Earl of Clanricarde looked at John, his second son, and now the tears poured unheeded down into his beard.

The moment of surprise and uncertainty was over. Sir Henry Sidney had not stirred, giving no sign that what he had just witnessed might be one of the most important moments of his mission to Ireland. The soldiers had wakened to their duty, and when both swords were safely on the altar there was a sharp command. The two brothers at the steps were surrounded by russet coats and the gleam of armor. The soldiers took them out through the vestry to avoid the people, and their father watched them go, collapsing then into his seat as if he had in the moment lost the usage of his legs.

Across the aisle, Grainne watched with eyes as dark as peat pools, and beside her Richard Burke sat rigid in his iron vest and did not dare to look at her face. The two young De Burghes were not only companions in arms, but long-loved friends with whom she had shared her dreams for Ireland, and now she watched them lay down their swords for Ireland's sake. Dare he hope that she would do the same? He knew that a wrong word at this moment would set her in obstinacy more strong than ever, so he said nothing, and beside him Grainne stared ahead when it was over as though her darkened eyes could see nothing, but her sharp mind was as aware of his thoughts as if he spoke them aloud, and she would give him no satisfaction. The service was going on, and under cover of the wondering voices raised in an uncertain hymn she turned to him, her eyes again bright and blue.

"I would think they did it, Dick," she said, "because they were hungry. I would think a square meal would kill the pair of them."

Chapter 9

The congregation from the church moved out into a city whose population was wild with rumor and excitement as it milled through the streets, talking in small noisy knots, so that the soldiers had trouble in thrusting a passage through them for the lords and ladies. The shouting, arguing people could not agree. Some saw in the surrender of the wild Clanricardes the first real hope of peace for Connaught, and the first chance in their lifetime to face a certain future. Others saw it as the final tragic loss of their independence, and it was they who pushed and crowded to Grainne's stirrup as she rode through the press.

"Stand for Ireland, madam," they cried. "Stand for Ireland!"

"Queen Grainne for Ireland!"

"Fight for us, madam!"

Grainne looked down on them as her horse eased its way through, and took her yellow kirtle gently from their demanding hands, smiling at them since they looked to her, but her eyes were dark and distant as they had been when the Clanricarde swords were laid upon the altar. Patch rode behind her and listened to what they cried to her, and thought of what he had seen that morning; and thought back to the smoking desolation of the ravaged town of Athenry. Someone had to stop it, and now it was the fiercest Irish chiefs who had moved to do so. There would be peace across the green stony fields of Connaught, and chance for the rebuilt towns to stand without fresh flames roaring through their thatch, and for families to grow up without every boy rushing into the struggle as soon as he was strong enough to hold a sword. But for his family it was too late. There was nothing more, surely, that the Queen could do, and God knew she had done enough already, risking her own life and her husband's reputation. He looked ahead at the bright cavalcade and the crowded streets and saw them suddenly through a haze of weary tears.

It was that evening that Iron Dick was bidden to wait on Sir Henry Sidney in the long parlor of the huge gray stone house that was the residence of the Mayor of Galway. During the day, no word had passed between him and his wife about the surrender of her friends; anything he might have to say was firmly quelled by the grim, silencing look she turned on him at the smallest mention of their names. As dusk came creeping in from the sea to wrap the old gray city in between the rivers, he took his courage in his hands and faced her in the warm shadows of her parlor.

"Do you come with me this evening, madam, or do you not?" He was past diplomacy and careful talk.

Patch watched them from behind the high back of the Queen's chair, looking from closed face to closed face. Neither would speak out, although Richard Burke most obviously longed to beg her in this last moment to do as her young friends had done that morning, and give her name for Ireland and for peace; and Grainne looked at him across the glowing fire, her face sharp and thin, saying nothing to answer him at all.

"Did I not say, my husband," she said in deliberate evasion, "that I would come with you to bear you company?"

Richard Burke lifted hopeless hands, as if to say that that was not enough and well she knew it, and his baffled eyes locked with hers, bright and enigmatic in the firelight. He shrugged then, a small, uncomfortable gesture in his iron vest, and turned away to the door.

"In that case," he said, and his voice showed nothing of his disappointment, "we had better make ourselves ready."

Grainne watched him until the door was closed on his back, and then with an impatient gesture she seized her snuffbox, sniffing angrily and clumsily at the dark brown powder so that it scattered down her bodice. She snapped the gold lid shut between her fingers and became suddenly aware of Patch behind her, beyond the candles and the firelight. She wheeled on him, leaning around the carved back of her chair.

"And what would you do, Patrick O'Flaherty?" she demanded. "And what would you do?" Her eyes blazed at him in anger and defiance, and yet somehow they were pleading, and the boy stared back at her, unhappily aware of a turmoil of suffering and emotion that he was too young to understand. His heart ached for her, for he was not too young to know that she was torn in two between her wild love of adventure, and her ships, and her lonely island kingdom that was her own with no one to tell her yea or nay; torn between these things and peace for Ireland, and all the small people in it who were not her own, but who were Irish like herself and had the same need to live.

"What would you do?" she blazed at him, and looked him up and down as if he were the object of her personal fury, but this time Patch felt no need to run away, for he was gaining the measure of this strange, wild woman, so far from the stately Queen he had imagined, and he knew her need of someone to shout at for the moment. But he could give her no answer, and after a few seconds of furious silence she answered her own question, her thin face twisted with contempt. "Ah," she said, "I forgot you are a soft one! You would pluck the English from the very sea and bring them home and waste good food on them! I would know, O'Flaherty, what you would do! Well do not count on it," she shouted, "neither you nor that long miserable bar of iron that is my husband! Stand for Ireland, they shouted to me in the streets today, with Ulick and John laying their swords upon an English altar. Stand for Ireland! And who will, if I do not? Who would lead them now?"

Still he had no answer to give her, and as she looked at him, the anger gradually faded from her face and she looked thin and white and tired. Patch remembered her wounded shoulder and felt sick with his desire to help her, but he could find no word.

"I trouble you, O'Flaherty," she said then wearily, "with matters too big for that shock head of yours. Go get me Honor, and tell her I am ready to put on my finery for my English evening."

Patch paused at the door as he went out and looked back

at her, her chin sunk in her hands and her elbows planted on her spread knees, eyes dark and brooding on the fire, from where the red glow spread across the sadness of her ugly face. He had a sudden feeling that she was like one of the dancing bears that he had seen in the market place in Athenry; a wild thing, caught and tied in this splendid house, when she should be rocking to the lift of the waves with her bare feet spread on the deck that was her own, her men about her and her black hair lifting to the wind. Deeply and helplessly he sighed and turned along the gallery to the stairs to search for Honor.

When it came to the evening, she was ready before Iron Dick, standing in the glowing hall to wait for him with conscious patience, the firelight, soft on her crimson kirtle, painting shadows down the snow-white folds of her cloak. A great ancient brooch from the days of the Kings held it like a dagger across her throat, and there was gold gleaming in her hair and at her wrists, heavy and old as the folds of her mountains. On her feet were the new shoes, bright crimson satin stitched with pearls, planted one beside the other on the polished floor, as though she dared anyone to say she could not walk in them. Close behind her stood her page, scrubbed and groomed by Honor till his eyes smarted and his head sang, and his ears, crimson with washing, stood out from the sides of his well-brushed head.

The hall was crowded; all the family of the Burkes gathered to see their Mayo chief make the history of their tribe, full of self-righteousness that what they did was done for Ireland. They were to ride behind the M'William Eughter through the streets to the Mayor's house, to show the citizens of Galway that their chief was not alone in this pact with England, but had all the power and arms of his tribe behind him. They looked to prosperity when peace was made, and safety for their lands and castles and great houses; and the long hall was full of the high, pleased murmur of people who had no doubts of what they did, or of themselves; warm with self-congratulation. Heads were high above white sparkling ruffs, and plumed caps nodded their bright feathers over bland, smiling faces. Only Queen Grainne stood alone, her forbidding eyes telling all Burkes to keep their distance; saying clearly that anything she did, she did alone, and wanted none of them. When Iron Dick came down the stairs to the bows and smiles of all the leaders of his tribe, she stood still in silence and looked at him above their respectful heads, and he had no eyes for anyone but her. But now he would not ask her anything.

"Madam," he said, and his voice was stiff as his ironbound bow, with the pale velvet of his doublet creasing neatly over the metal hinges. "Madam, I did not know whether to expect you here."

In silence she held out a hand for him to take, and only as they moved off through the bowing crowd did she slide her blue eyes sideways at him.

"Did I not tell you," she hissed, "that I would come to bear you company? Now unless you wish me shame you before all your tribe, lend me a strong arm for these shoes will never hold my feet! God send me my bare soles again with all speed, and a good firm piece of deck to put them on, for I am like to throw myself at the lord Sidney's feet from the top of these heels!"

Behind her Patch caught her words and bent his head to hide the grin on his face as she lurched along the polished floor, with her husband holding to her tightly as he could, and turning his stiff, inclining face from side to side to acknowledge his relations.

Through the torchlit streets the crowds were silent, pressed back against the houses to let the cavalcade of riders pass, but, like Iron Dick, they had eyes only for the white-cloaked figure at its head with the torchlight flickering on the gold in her black hair; as if they knew she held their future in her long hands; knew, and trusted her.

The great train of Burkes was left outside in the courtyard at the Mayor's house; the stone flags rattled with crowded, restless hooves, and the white breath of their horses rose to the first cool air of autumn, above their velvet caps and nodding plumes. Grainne looked strangely alone, as she stood above their brilliance in the plain clothes of her islands, indifferent to them all, but insisting that her page should stay with her, right into the presence of the Lord Deputy.

"An' if your Queen Elizabeth came to visit me," she demanded fiercely of the Chamberlain who tried to keep Patch out, "wouldn't she be welcome to bring her page to my very fireside!"

The man stood back at once, as much shocked at her suggestion as agreeable to what she asked, and Grainne seized the moment to sweep past him through the wide flung doors, with a clattering rush of the new heels and her grinning page following close behind. At the foot of the great staircase she came to an abrupt halt, and her embarrassed husband looked down at her in anguished patience.

"O'Flaherty," she hissed. "Come up close behind me."

Patch came, conscious of the pained face of Iron Dick who was doing his best to pretend that nothing was amiss.

"O'Flaherty! I have lost one of these devil's shoes. Put out a foot and kick it close under my skirts."

Patch could feel her husband stiffen with outrage, but they

both knew better than to argue with Grainne. Carefully, keeping his disinterested face turned straight in front of him, he reached out and felt for the wandering shoe, tipped it right way up, and gave it a gentle kick so that it vanished under the crimson folds of the Queen's skirts.

" 'Tis there, madam," he whispered, and standing straight and dignified as became a Queen, Grainne gave a small shuffle and a gracious smile spread across her ugly face.

"I'll reward you with an earldom, Patrick," she grinned, and proceeded to lead her speechless husband on toward the stairs, smiling and inclining her head to the assembled people with all the regal dignity of Elizabeth herself.

Outside the door where the Lord Deputy was to receive them, Iron Dick had need to stop and draw out his fine kerchief to mop his brow, but he had no words to say to her, and she in turn turned on him her most brilliant smile. He shook his head helplessly, and prayed that she would not, on this of all evenings, give way to some wild prank that might damage the cause of Ireland for years to come.

Sir Henry Sidney sat beside the fire in a high-backed chair of gilded leather, looking even more slight and gentle than he had done in the church, his forehead high and mild and intelligent below his soft brown hair. His legs in hose of violet silk were stretched out easily to the fire, and there were but two other gentlemen in the room with him, apart from the servants who stood beside the doors. His alert eyes went immediately to the tall woman who came in, and he got up from his chair with great courtesy, saying something in English to the man beside him, who spoke to Queen Grainne in Gaelic.

"Sir Henry Sidney begs your pardon, ma'am, that he holds so close to the fire, but he finds your damp country cold. He begs you now, to come close yourself and be seated."

"I am well enough where I am, thank his good lordship," Grainne answered from her place inside the door. "The damp winds of this country, like everything else in it, are familiar to me, and I do not heed them." It was not said discourteously, but as a simple statement of fact that made it clear she was not going to move another step, and Patch, with instant insight, knew that she had lost another shoe. There was a long moment of awkwardness, for Iron Dick could not leave her where she was and move forward, and Grainne, with a bland disinterested face, waited for what might happen next. There was silence in the room and the fire crackled and glowed on the rich paneled walls and the velvet hangings; a small dog turned himself over lazily on the warm tiles of the hearth, while Iron Dick perspired quietly and did not know what to do, and cursed the moment he had ever thought it wise to bring her. In the end, the Lord Deputy sat down again, easily.

"Well, madam will forgive me," he said through his interpreter, "if I stay near the fire."

Madam smiled as amiably as ever, and Patch could see her fishing about underneath her skirts. Then Iron Dick cleared his throat and took as much of a step in front of her as he dared. There was nothing to be done but conduct the interview across the long space of polished wood between the fireplace and the door. The interpreter consulted a parchment in his hand, and spoke to him in Gaelic.

"Who are you," he said formally, although the parchment had told him all of this. "Who are you, and of what county and what tribe?"

Iron Dick bent himself from the waist in a bow as formal and restricted as the limits of his iron vest, ignoring the man, and speaking to the Lord Deputy.

"Non sum homo eruditionis inscius," he said in excellent Latin. "Si lingua Latina uti vis facillime colloqui poterimus." (*I am not a man deficient in learning. If you wish to use the Latin language, we will be able to speak very easily.*)

Sir Henry Sidney's eyes warmed at once, and he sat more upright in his chair. A great part of his difficulty in settling the woes of this troubled country lay in the fact that he could not speak straight to a man's face and understand him. Also, he was himself a great scholar, and took pleasure in using the ancient tongues.

"Dic mihi igitur," he answered. "Dic mihi statim et quis sis et quam regionem habited et qua ex gente ortus sis. Magnopere enim gaudoe quod colloqui possumus." (*Then tell me directly, therefore, who you are, and of what county and out of what tribe. For I rejoice greatly that we are able to speak.*)

"Nomen mihi est Richard Burke. Servio Elizabethae, reginae maximae. Princeps sum omnium quibus nomen est Burkes et qui familias paulo minarum ducit." (*My name is Richard Burke. I serve her Majesty, Queen Elizabeth. I am Chieftain of all who have the name Burke and he who leads some of the lower tribes.*)

The formal sentences flowed on as Iron Dick professed his loyalty to Elizabeth of England in the name of all his tribes, and in token surrendered all his lands in Ireland to her Crown. Sir Henry Sidney listened quietly. All the time he sat immobile, his long hands stretched on the carved arms of his chair, but he could not keep his eyes from flickering over to the tall, dark woman who had not moved from her place inside the door, her blue eyes hard and bright as sapphires on his face, as though she wished to read what kind of man he was. No mention had been made of her, nor of whom she was, though Sir Henry Sidney knew well. He had been fiercely conscious of her across from him in the silent church that morning, sitting with her proud face while her two friends had given up their swords. One of the most important things with which his Queen had charged him was to seek out this pirate lady.

"She calls herself a Queen, even as I. Tame her, or defeat her," Elizabeth had said. "This I charge you, my lord Sidney, for as she is, she is but a thorn in my side, making a mock of me before all the world, and lending help to all my enemies."

Now as Richard Burke's steady voice droned on, he watched her across the room and found her little like the wild and brutal savage of the stories. She stood silent by the door, and that in itself he found strangely humble. Mild and quiet she looked in her crimson gown, save only for these strange, brilliant eyes that never left his own face. Close behind her stood a lanky fair-haired page, who never lifted his eyes from the floor at her feet. Was she truly going to let her husband do all her talking for her? From all that he had heard, she was not usually at a loss for words.

With a small start, he realized that Richard Burke had come to the end of all he had to say, bowing stiffly as he offered the complete surrender of all his lands. With only a spare thought to wonder if it were true that he always went cased in steel beneath his doublet,

Sir Henry Sidney gave him his full attention summoning Latin as beautiful and precise as the chieftain's own.

"Her Gracious Majesty will not ask this sacrifice of you," he said, knowing all there was to know of Iron Dick before he had ever opened his mouth in this lamplit room. "She knows you for her loyal and faithful servant, and returns you all your lands in her name, as a token of her esteem for you and for your service. She also bids me in her name to make you offer of a knighthood, naming you Sir Richard Burke of Mayo."

All of Iron Dick's long, sheeplike face flushed red with pleasure, and he bowed again to the creaking limits of his iron vest, protesting that too much honor was allowed him. Sir Henry Sidney glanced across the room, fully expecting to see the same pleasure echoed on his wife's face, for surely she should be proud to be the lady Burke. To his amazement and amusement, for there was something in this fine, silent woman with the flashing eyes that appealed to him, he saw that she was struggling on the edge of laughter, looking at her respectful husband with a face of wild hilarity, eyes blazing with amusement, and one long, hooked tooth showing suddenly across her lower lip.

She looked across only at her husband.

"She did well, the woman Elizabeth," she said to him in Gaelic, "to make a lady Burke out of a Queen as good as herself. Who is she, the creature, to give me a title!" Iron Dick's flush of pleasure turned to the scarlet of anguish, and the interpreter stared from one to the other, white with shock.

"What did madam say?" asked Sir Henry, fascinated at the play of expressions on the three faces, but the man gibbered helplessly and would not say. Before he could find words for anything else, Grainne turned to him with her voice ringing in the paneled parlor as clear as if she gave orders on her own decks.

"My compliments to the lord Sidney," she said, "and tell him that I am Grainne O'Malley, Queen of the Islands and Chieftain in my own right of the Barony of Murrisk, and I send my greetings to his mistress as one Queen to another." She paused, and for a moment the watching men saw her face grow deadly sad as if she knew a brief space of intolerable grief that, like her smile, brought her ugly face to a strange and sudden beauty. Then into the silence she cried, "And tell him that I have two hundred fighting men, and thirty ships with their sailors, and ask him if his Queen could use them. If she can, then the woman is welcome to them at my hands."

Iron Dick turned to her so sharply that he was brought to a painful halt by the unyielding limits of his vest, but it did nothing to dim the glow of mixed delight and exasperation on his face. The shocked interpreter could do no more than shrug his red satin shoulders and translate what she had said. Sir Henry Sidney held his breath, feeling as though he had caught a wild and valuable bird, that rested now a moment in his hand, but one false move or hasty step and he could lose it. Quietly he stood up and bowed to her.

"Madam," he said, "this is more than either she or I had dared to hope for. Will you not come closer and seat yourself, and we can talk over these things, as my Gracious Majesty would wish." The Mayor of Galway stared from one to the other as if his well-ordered world were coming to its end.

For a minute, Grainne looked at the Lord Deputy from her shadows, her eyes blazing and her whole face alight with a devilment that filled her husband with terror and alarm. Then she whipped up the hem of her crimson kirtle, and the one shoe on her foot went flying across the room past the shattered face of the Mayor, to hit the paneling with a thump and fall below it to the floor. The other one, she had to find, feeling around the floor until it followed the first one with a well aimed kick, and then she turned to the blinking Sir Henry with a radiant and satisfied grin.

"God's truth, my lord," she said bluntly, "I could think of nothing with those objects twisting the bones of my feet!" She gestured imperiously to the gaping Mayor. "Bring me a chair now, my good fellow, for my lord Sidney and I must talk business." She stretched her stockinged feet out to the fire and wriggled her released toes with pleasure, scrabbling in her pocket for her snuffbox. Over her pinched fingers and the tumbling brown grains that already marked her snow-white cloak, she glared suddenly at her husband and at the Mayor, who had been startled into bringing her a chair as if he was her servant, and who now stood bitterly regretting it with his hands folded on his thin stomach and his long face above his enameled chain folded into every shape of disapproval.

"Out, all of you!" cried Grainne. "Think you that I will discuss the affairs of queens before half Galway! Leave me alone with my lord Sidney. *Sir*," she emphasized the title with a wild hoot of laughter, "Sir Richard Burke is not the only one who has received an education, and I have enough Latin to gain all I want. Patrick O'Flaherty," she added as an afterthought, "do you pick up those shoes for we might get a good price for them from someone who has use for such things."

Doing his best to stifle his laughter, Patch crept round the walls and picked up the red satin shoes, and then bowed himself out the door, followed by the indignant interpreter and the outraged Mayor, and finally Iron Dick, who glanced back apprehensively at his lady wife. Patch well understood his fears. But the face of Sir Henry Sidney across the fire was warm and amused, as though he much welcomed the cool, fresh breath of the sea that had come into his overheated parlor to blow away the formal manners and fine words, and allow two people to face each other and try in honesty to settle at least one corner of this turbulent, exhausted Ireland.

Patch took up his station at the end of the wide gallery to wait for her, and he alone saw her coming towards him some hour later, a fistful of parchments in her hand. There was nothing left of her fine hilarity. She did not see him as she came, and her face was naked to her sacrifice, showing one moment of agonized understanding of what she had given up. And what, he wondered, had been her terms? What price had she asked Sir Henry Sidney for the gift of her pride and independence? He had a sick, certain knowledge of what it might be, and suddenly felt very cold, and angry too, that he should be thrust all unwillingly into things, like these, that were none of his affair. As she came abreast of him, she saw him and stopped.

"Well, Patrick O'Flaherty," she said, and he tried to keep his eyes from the tears that traced her cheeks. "Well, now are you satisfied? There should be no more killing for the soft ones like yourself!"

Patch shifted from one foot to the other, his eyes glued to the parchments in her hands, and he wanted to shout at her not to make him take all the blame.

"It was you, madam, or your men, who killed these men, not me! I did not even steal the sheep!" And now she filled him with guilt, making him feel she had surrendered her kingdom simply to save his family, for what were these documents under the Lord Deputy's seal, if not a pardon for his parents. She followed his eyes and snatched at one of them.

"There then," she cried. "Take it!" She thrust it into his hands. "Take it to the jail and get them out, and take them back to their bit of land, and long may they settle! You will go with them?"

"Yes madam." He did not think closely of what he said, puzzled as to the other parchments which she still held close. Again she read his thoughts and brandished them in his face.

"Did you think the O'Flahertys were the only stone on the mountain? Did you think I would bargain with my lord Sidney for them alone? You do yourself too much honor, Patrick! The O'Flahertys are as nothing, nothing! Do you not understand that I have other friends and other loyalties since long before that accursed night I fell across an O'Flaherty in a bog!" He felt the weight of guilt pour away from him in a sweet stream of happiness, for he had forgotten the two young men who had come into the church that morning. She had treated with Sir Henry Sidney for them, and for Ireland, and the O'Flahertys were indeed nothing, but they would be free.

"Not, madam," he tried to stammer. "Not that I am not grateful, but I was troubled. I was troubled . . ."

"You were troubled that I had bartered my kingdom for a mess of O'Flahertys, and you did not think it worth the bargain. It troubled your conscience?"

He nodded dumbly.

"I am glad you have one." Her sardonic face grew serious, and the dark blue eyes were sad on his face.

"I have bartered my kingdom, Patrick O'Flaherty, because even you kept telling me that it was the best thing I could do for Ireland. And if we get a few O'Flahertys and others from the jails as we go, then that is all to the good."

He moved from one foot to the other, and could not take his eyes from the parchments. Her eyes were still sad, reading his mind.

"You cannot wait to go?"

"No, madam." He could not be dishonest with her.

There were ladies and gentlemen behind her, waiting to bring her to supper. He was filled with sadness to leave her, but the pardon was like a live coal in his hand.   *

"Go then," she said. "Go now. And when you get them, do not come back. Go back with them to Coolinbawn or wherever it is you live."

He looked at her, alarm all over his fair face. This was too sudden. He could not leave her as easily as this.

"Go," she said firmly. "Go to your family, for there is not room for both of us with you." She smiled at him brilliantly as though he were some fine lord that she had just met, and then she turned away into the company. "I come, my lords," she said. "I had a small business to settle with the boy."

Patch stood a moment, his bright urgency fled, but he knew that she was right. If he went home with his family now, he must sever himself from the wild, outlawed life of the Queen's men, and settle down again upon his father's farm. It was true. There was no place for both these ways of life, and how often had he said that she should make peace just so that people like himself should be able to live and prosper quietly on their farmlands, without fear that battle might at any moment snatch their homes and even their children's lives. Now she offered him this very safety in his father's house, so why then did he feel suddenly bereft and grief-stricken, as though it were only second best? He shook himself and reminded himself of the pardon in his hands, and doubt fled; with it he fled himself, out into the cool, crowded streets where the people still flocked in the moonlight, resisting all efforts at curfew, discussing the overwhelming events of their day. Patch fled along among them, stopping to listen to nothing, dodging between their legs and in and out through the arguing groups, until he came to an abrupt halt as he crashed into someone who came flying from a side alley almost as fast as he ran himself.

"Graves of the saints!" cried a voice, and even as he gasped for his lost breath, Patch peered with astonishment into the face of the man above him.

"James!" he gasped. "James!"

"Graves of the saints," said the voice again, and a hand took the boy by the hair and turned his face to the moonlight. Patch squinted at the red-bearded face in the shadows.

"James, it's me! Patch! I knew you at once! No one else says graves of the saints like that. James, where have you been, you have been long away!"

His eldest brother kept a grip on his hair, and his voice was astonished.

"Well you all know where I have been," he said. "I have been fighting with my lord Ulick of Clanricarde. I came into the city with him today, and I have a free pardon like all his men. But you ask, young one, where I have been. Where, by the graves of these very saints, have you been these long weeks? Young Sean Rohan had some unlikely tale whispered in the deadest secrecy, of dead men and Queen Grainne? What is it all about?"

Patch had no time to spare for his own story.

"Oh James, I have a pardon for them! Come with me to the jail and we can get them out, and then I will tell you all my story."

"Get who out?" James was genuinely puzzled.

"The family!" Patch banged the big chest in front of him in his urgency. "They are in the jail here, and I have a pardon for them."

"Then they made a swift journey there, for I left them yesterday well in their own home, and with no thought of going back to jail, but only to rebuild the house and settle things again as fast as possible."

"All of them?" In the cool, white light Patch stared at him and his mouth opened and closed. "All of them?"

"All of them except you," James said, trying to see Patch's face, sensing his desperate bewilderment that left him almost collapsed, unable to say a word.

"Here now, come, young one," he said. "We have a bit of talking to do. I'll keep away from the middle of the city if you don't mind, for there's some don't care for us who have followed my lords John and Ulick, pardon or no pardon."

He took Patch by the arm, and did not stop marching the bewildered boy until they were clear out along the edges of the quays, the great walls of the city rising behind them, and the moonlight gleaming over the shining width of the bay.

"God grant the Watch doesn't find us here," James said, and they settled behind a heap of casks, the dark sea swelling and slapping below them on the ancient stones. "Now you tell me everything you've done," he said, and instantly Patch launched on his tale, the parchment turning and crackling between his fingers. In the half light, he could feel his brother's astonished eyes on his face as he went on.

"Graves of the saints," James said inevitably at the end. "And you are here now in Galway with Queen Grainne?"

"Yes," said Patch proudly, delighted to be able to impress his eldest brother. "At least," he added lamely, "I was."

"What do you mean, 'was'?"

"Well, I told her I was going to get my family and go home."

He sensed there was something not quite right, and looked anxiously up at James.

"Can I not go home?"

"Graves of the saints," said his brother yet again, reflecting on the whole strange story. "What a tale, by all that's holy! But you can't go home."

"Why not, if they are all there? James, I beg you, tell me all you know."

"They're all there in truth. But, young one, that soldier who crawled out of the bog lived long enough to be shown our father, and he said that he had never seen him in his life before, and if that was Patrick O'Flaherty, it was not the man who had stolen the sheep. That was a lad, he says, and our father plays quiet and never says he has another son. With all this forgiveness flying about, and only honest criminals in the jails, they let them all go, but i'faith, young one, you had still better not go home. Some English soldier might hear of another Patrick O'Flaherty come back, and I think all the forgiveness would go flying out the casement."

"But I want to go home! And I did nothing."

James looked at him curiously and shrugged. Months of living the rough, outlawed life of the Clanricardes had taught him that one place was much the same as any other.

"You've done well enough these last months without a home," he said. "I am away back now for a while to settle down and help our father, for I have an official pardon remember, so I am safe. Can you not go back to your Queen?"

Patch hung his head, and breathed deeply the warm, tarry smell of the casks behind them. How could he go back? He had almost run away from her.

"She's surrendered to the English," he said inconsequently, and James threw back his red head and laughed aloud, stifling it at once for fear he should be heard.

"I'll believe that," he said sardonically, as if it were the unlikeliest jest he had ever heard. "I'll believe that when I see it!"

"She has! I know she has. She . . ." He stopped abruptly, overwhelmed by his recollection of the sad and lonely woman he had seen struggling with her decision. How could he tell of her surrender for the sake of Ireland to the gay, roving James, who took the sword for fun and went wherever he could find a fight.

"She means well, the wild woman," James went on. "She means well, and she loves us all, every one of us. But she's like myself, God save her, she can never resist the smell of a fight."

Patch was silent, unable to answer for he had not grown up sufficiently to find the words; but he stared out over the dark, shining sea, where the gibbous moon hung like a great lamp above the mountains and he knew that he had grown up enough to understand a little. He had lost all his foolish dreams about a fair and stately Queen, walking through her castle in a golden diadem, passing gentle words with those about her, strong and severe and dignified when necessary. He had gained instead—he knew suddenly in the moment when James had laughed—a desperate loyalty to this wild, wayward, and capricious creature who was in truth Queen Grainne, and he knew now that no matter what she did in the future, it would be right for him.

"Yes," he said to his brother, and it was all that he could say, "she loves us. I am going back." It was not, he realized, so hard not to go home. He had been a long time away, most of his life in fact, and his deep roots were not there. "I am going back," he said again, already standing up with his face toward the center of the city.

Queen Grainne and her husband were alone in the parlor when he knocked timidly on the door, and the stiff voice of Iron Dick bade him enter. Iron Dick looked anything but pleased to see him, and moved as if to tell him go, but

Grainne lifted a hand, and then she watched in absolute silence as Patch advanced, redfaced, into the middle of the floor. She gave him no help at all, her face expressionless and her eyes on him, waiting.

"Madam," he managed to say at last, into a silence that seemed to boom in his ears like thunder. "Madam, I have come back."

"So," she said, and that was all.

Finding his voice from some uncomfortable place around the middle of his throat, he stumbled through the tale of his meeting with James, and of the pardon that was never needed. He saw her blink sharply a couple of times, but her face did not change.

"And so you came back here as second best?"

"No, madam." Suddenly his nervousness left him, and he lifted his head to face her, saying something that he had only just discovered for himself. "No, madam," he said. "I would have come back anyway." He smiled broadly, knowing in the instant that this was true and, at that same moment, Grainne's grim face broke up and she began to laugh, long and loud, throwing back her head to roll her hair loose on the high back of her chair; startling her dogs out of their sleep. She banged her palms on her knees.

"God's death," she gasped, "but I will tell until my own grave the story of how I nearly got myself killed getting the O'Flaherty family out of Galway jail when they were never there at all! Owen got himself well misinformed! Well, Patrick O'Flaherty, you owe me much to have made such a fool of me before all my people. Will you serve me truly now, to make up for it, and no more of your 'Madam, I must leave you,' but be a man, and stick to what you put your hand to?"

Patrick remembered James laughing about her down on

the quay, and made a last desperate bid to be quite sure of her; quite sure that things were as he thought.

"Yes madam, I will serve you," he said gravely, and then added hopefully, "but now you have made peace with England, we should not be fighting with them on the seas, should we?" He recalled his Queen those hours back in the Mayor's house, with tears wet on her cheeks and her kingdom given up for Ireland.

"We *are* at peace with England, madam?" he asked urgently. Grainne glared at him.　*

"Did I not say so?"

For the first time, Iron Dick, Sir Richard Burke, spoke directly to his wife's page, looking at him across the fire with sad, pouchy eyes.

"I wouldn't like to count on it, boy," he said. "I wouldn't like to count on it."

Between them, Queen Grainne looked from one to the other and stretched her bare feet out to the fire, her snuffbox clinking in her fingers, and her eyes were very blue and very bright and filled with devilment.

What Parts of This Story are True
and What Happened Next

Grainne was a real person who made her living by piracy off the northwest coast of Ireland in the sixteenth century. She was married first to Donal Flaherty, and then after he died, to Richard Burke. She lived in the Burke castle of Carraigahowley or Rockfleet as well as in her own O'Malley castle on Clare Island. She did in fact meet with Lord Sidney in 1576 and promise her allegiance, but as her husband suspected, it didn't last long. Just a few weeks after that meeting, she attacked Desmund in Munster, was arrested and kept in jail until 1579.

After she was released, she and her husband Richard Burke engaged in wars of succession among the local clans. It was only then that he claimed the title M'William (MacWilliam) which Ms Polland gives him throughout this story.

In 1584, Richard Bingham was named provincial president of Connacht and while his superior, Sir John Perrot, wanted to deal in peace with the clans, Bingham believed that the Irish could only be tamed by the sword. When Richard Burke died, Bingham gave the title of MacWilliam to another clan instead of to the son of Richard Burke and Grainne. The Burkes then rose up in rebellion. In 1587 Bingham was called away to fight in Spain and Grace appealed to Sir John Perrot, gaining a pardon and regaining her lands lost in fighting with Bingham.

When Bingham returned to Ireland he unleashed a relentless battle against Graine and her son, Tibbot-na-Long, who finally submitted. Fearing that Tibbot would be executed without a trial, Grainne traveled to England to meet with Queen Elizabeth herself. As a result of their historic meeting, Queen Elizabeth restored all of Grainne's property, recmmended that her son be released, and ordered that taxes on her son's property be diverted to a pension for Grainne.

This enraged Richard Bingham and he continued his harrassment of her, including ordering troops to be stationed on her lands which she had to support. Grainne set out for London to appeal to Queen Elizabeth again, and Richard Bingham, fearing the charges against him, fled to England and was imprisoned.

Continually harrassed by Red Hugh O'Donnell, Grainne's son Tibbot finally sided with the English Crown. His life was also incredibly fascinating and you might be interested to do more research about him to learn more about this time in Irish history. By 1603, Ireland was completely under English control.

Left without means, Grainne reverted to the way she knew best to provide for her family. The last record of her was in 1601 when an English warship recorded an encounter: "a galley I met . . . she rowed with thirty oars and had on board . . . 100 good shot . . . This galley comes out of Connacht and belongs to Grace O'Malley."

Grainne is believed to have died in 1603. While her true life is mostly shrouded in mystery, she remains a folk hero and legendary defender of true Ireland. Ms. Polland's story is one of many literary, romantic views of the enigmatic Grainne, and we are honored to reprint it for a new generation of readers.

M. Davidson, 2020

Granuaile's Castle on Clare Island

Rockfleet or Carrigahowley Castle of the Bourke's